Friends or Foes?

DANE HAD BEEN BY FAR THE MOST OUTSPOKEN CRITIC of the Alliance all term. Less than half an hour ago, Aerin, herself, had accused him of failing to value the freedom he had here.

She slowed her steps, then pressed her head against the rough bark of a tree at the garden's edge. That first day of classes she had been a pawn, afraid of everything, and based on one conversation, she had made a snap judgment about a young man she really knew nothing about. Hadn't that also been part of today's discussion? Dane telling her she knew nothing about him. Yes, just before he threatened her.

And tried to save her life.

Even now she could feel the intensity of Dane's grip. If she had fallen, that grip would have stopped her. It had been that tight, that fierce. It had not been warm, or polite, or halfhearted in any way. It had squeezed her knuckles together in almost bone-cracking pain, and it would have held her up.

Maybe he had not meant to threaten her.

Or maybe he had.

Other Books You May Enjoy

Academy 7

ANNE OSTERLUND

speak

An Imprint of Penguin Group (USA) Inc.

SPEAK
Published by the Penguin Group
Penguin Group (USA) Inc., 345 Hudson Street, New York, New York 10014, U.S.A.
Penguin Group (Canada), 90 Eglinton Avenue East, Suite 700, Toronto, Ontario, Canada M4P 2Y3
(a division of Pearson Penguin Canada Inc.)
Penguin Books Ltd, 80 Strand, London WC2R 0RL, England
Penguin Ireland, 25 St Stephen's Green, Dublin 2, Ireland
(a division of Penguin Books Ltd)
Penguin Group (Australia), 250 Camberwell Road, Camberwell, Victoria 3124, Australia
(a division of Pearson Australia Group Pty Ltd)
Penguin Books India Pvt Ltd, 11 Community Centre,
Panchsheel Park, New Delhi - 110 017, India
Penguin Group (NZ), 67 Apollo Drive, Rosedale, North Shore 0632, New Zealand
(a division of Pearson New Zealand Ltd.)
Penguin Books (South Africa) (Pty) Ltd, 24 Sturdee Avenue,
Rosebank, Johannesburg 2196, South Africa

Registered Offices: Penguin Books Ltd, 80 Strand, London WC2R 0RL, England

Published by Speak, an imprint of Penguin Group (USA) Inc., 2009

1 3 5 7 9 10 8 6 4 2

LIBRARY OF CONGRESS CATALOGING-IN-PUBLICATION DATA
Osterlund, Anne.
Academy 7 / Anne Osterlund.
p. cm.
Summary: Aerin Renning and Dane Madousin struggle as incoming students at
the most exclusive academy in the Universe, both hiding secrets that are too painful to reveal,
not realizing that those very secrets link them together.
ISBN 978-0-14-241437-8 (pbk. : alk. paper)
[1. Science fiction. 2. Emotional problems--Fiction. 3. Fathers--Fiction. 4. Schools--Fiction.] I. Title.
II. Title: Academy seven.
PZ7.O8454Ac 2009
[Fic]--dc22
2008041323

Speak ISBN 978-0-14-241437-8

Printed in the United States of America

For Maria—
who defines the word *friendship*

And for Andy, Filipp, and Marcus,
and all the other young men who push buttons and
boundaries and have the potential to change the universe

Acknowledgments

Thank you to my parents for letting me invade their basement to write; to my best friend, Maria, whose artistic talent is responsible for my web design, postcards, etc; to Elaine, Jan, Orice, Shirley, and Maria for reading drafts and providing feedback; to Dawn, who is responsible for the technical side of my Web site and is very patient with my lack of technological expertise; to the amazing people at Penguin who have been so supportive despite my dearth of published credentials, and to Angelle who took a huge chance on a princess who should not be a princess and a writer who has never been very good at staying inside the box. Neither *Academy 7* nor *Aurelia* would exist without all of these tremendous people. And thank you to all the students, friends, librarians, teachers, co-workers, parents, and bookstore workers who have been so supportive on this crazy learning curve.

Contents

Academy 7

Prologue: FUGITIVE

Aerin tried to ignore the bloodstain on the control panel of the *Fugitive*. Her father's ship. And his blood. She thrust the image away, cramming it into the small chest at the back of her mind, then slamming shut the lid. *Enough memories.*

The aged ship rattled as though its exterior had hit turbulence, but the cockpit window showed only the clear black emptiness of space sprinkled with distant stars. Aerin checked the fuel. The dial remained in the same slot it had been in when she had taken off hours before. As did the arrow on the pressure monitor.

The rattle grew more intense, every piece of the former trade ship seeming to move. Metal sheeting wobbled back and forth on rounded screws. Exposed wires trembled from open patches in the wall. Cords swung from the ceiling.

The message was clear. She was not going to make it. Not to the next planet. Not even to the next space station. If only the ship's computer would tell her what was wrong. Then she might be able to fix it. But though the autopilot functioned well enough to complete takeoff and follow a course, the screen remained a sullen blank.

The hasty repairs she had completed in her final moments on Vizhan had been enough to get the rickety ship off the ground, through the atmosphere, and into space. They were not going to be enough to save her life. Not without help.

Mouthing a silent plea, she switched on the radio. A green light glowed. *Thank you,* she whispered in her mind, then turned the volume dial with shaking fingers. A soft hum grew louder. Working! At least it sounded like it was working.

Aerin typed in the code for the distress signal. *Beep, beep, beep, beeeep, beeeep, beeeep, beep, beep, beep*—the code entered the machine and began repeating the same message over and over.

She tucked her bare feet beneath her and slumped back in her chair. Nothing she could do now. Just keep the ship aimed for the coordinates marked in the logbook as those of the nearest space station and hope someone came out of the vast void.

Her eyelids grew heavy with the weight of exhaustion. Perhaps it would be better just to crawl into one of the ship berths, her father's since her own cot would now be too small for even the skinny limbs of her seventeen-year-old body.

Maybe she should just go to sleep. Let herself drift, thankful she would die free, here in her father's ship, as he had. Free from the hunger and violence of Vizhan. From the terror.

Fear is not the enemy. Love is—she recited the mantra that had kept her alive these past six years. Neither her conscience nor the ship's vibrating hull would let her rest. She would sit here, she knew, staring out the window, adjusting knobs and dials, fighting this cranky piece of machinery as long as she could.

Until help arrived or all breath left her body.

Time seemed not to move at all. Starlight failed to mark the passage of the hours, and the clock in the corner remained dark. She unscrewed the timepiece, then checked the tiny bulbs. The filaments were black. Broken. No surprise there. Far stronger objects had come apart during the crash.

Aerin fell back in her seat, once again staring into the distance. Waiting. For life. Or death. Her eyes on the window.

It was the radio, though, that finally brought hope. A crackling, then a faint voice through the static. Words fading in and out. Unrecognizable. Syllables lost in a netherworld without context.

She bent forward, snatching the mouthpiece. It came away in her hand, the cord severed. She hurled it and watched it bang off a wall, hit the floor, and skid fifteen feet to crash at the rear of the cabin.

The voice on the radio came again, yanking her back from frustration. The words grew stronger, clearer. "This is the *Envoy*, answering your distress call. Do you read?" The same message repeated over and over several times. She looked down at the radio, knowing there must be a way to respond in code.

But once again she fell victim to her own ignorance.

Still the voice did not give up. Instead, the message changed. "This is the *Envoy*, tracking a distress call at coordinates 09-74-6002. No verbal response received. Changing course to intercept call."

The voice faded and Aerin whispered the final sentence aloud, clutching at the words *intercept call*. Would the ship come then? To help? She waited, counting the seconds, aching for a sense of control.

Then the *Envoy* emerged, hundreds of feet of sleek blackness from nose to tail, its dark hull blending so thoroughly into space that it first made its presence known by blocking the starlight from her view. The vessel tilted toward her, pancake-flat edges outlining a pointed nose and wings that swept back from the sides like slick feathers on a fletched arrow. Then the ship rolled up, revealing a straight, narrow side.

Aerin's inner censor splintered the nerve endings in her brain. What had she done? Whom had she invited into her world? Her heart rattled at the same pace as the panels on the wall. She was caught, immobile, trapped in the spectrum of fear.

Chapter One
FIRE

Dane Madousin swept a rapid arc through the atmosphere, testing the speed of his new aircraft. The two-man ship cut a silent swath through the azure sky. "Sharp," Dane murmured to the machine, then flipped its light hull upside down.

His head dropped back, his gaze spotting the planet's surface. Chivalry's vast foliage stretched beneath him: fir and hemlock, maple and aspen, greenery tinged with reds and browns, split now and then by a ribbon of blue or, more often, a dry creek bed. *Pure nature,* Dane thought, wishing he had been assigned to this sector earlier.

He was sick of the artificial surface of the base and the tall skyscrapers of the planet's only city. Here was where the action was, where the blasting hot summer winds met with dry tinder and plenty of fuel. Prime conditions for a fire.

"I think we got something!" a boy's voice shrieked over the radio.

Dane turned down the volume. "Well, where is it?" he heard the fire chief say.

"Southeast quadrant," the boy said. "Looks like coordinates fifty-four by sixty-one."

Dane cocked his head, not bothering to check the map pinned to the visor. He knew the place was in his sector. "Let's go, *Gold Dust*," he said, flipping the aircraft right side up and punching in the coordinates.

"You got that, Madousin?" the chief's voice came again over the radio.

Dane picked up his mouthpiece. "Yeah, in motion," he said. *Finally.* Two summers flying old beaters with the company and nothing more exciting than a brushfire in City Park. Then this morning he had cashed in his savings for an interplanetary plane, and now, on the same day, had the chance for some action.

Not that the two were related. Dane knew the only reason he had been assigned to this sector was that the big blaze in the northwest required all the experienced fighters. Flyers under seventeen were usually kept in ad hoc, and he had another two weeks before crossing that milestone.

"What level of fire are we looking at?" asked the chief.

"Um, on the view screen the smoke looks black and kinda high," mumbled the boy.

That was helpful. Dane kept his sarcasm to himself. Being short on fighters meant the person running the monitors had next to no training.

"What type of material is burning?" the chief said in a patient voice.

"Trees?" the boy said.

"Trees around a house? Or a stream? Or a forest?" asked the adviser.

A damn forest, Dane got his answer through the cockpit window, not the radio. Black smoke billowed into the air, much too dark for a small stand of ground fuel. He grabbed for his mouthpiece. "I've got a forest fire blowing west, at least level three." He kept his voice calm as he had been trained, but his mind was screaming inside.

Stupid kid should never have let it near level three before calling in. This was not the kind of fire you could miss on your radar screen. Not if you were paying any kind of attention.

"Five planes in your radius. That going to provide enough support?" the chief asked.

By this time, ashes were pelting Dane's windshield, and he was thankful for the flame retardant that blocked out the smell of the smoke and kept the metal from scarring. He could see for certain now that the fire was out of control. Five planes were not going to cut it. They would be lucky even to make a dent. "We're going to need at least thirty planes here," Dane replied. "This thing has crowned."

"Crowned?" For the first time, the chief's voice faltered. "You're telling me the flames are out of the underbrush and burning leaves?"

"Needles. We're talking hundreds of fir and hemlock stretching far as the eye can see." Which was not all that far, considering the muffling gray haze filling the air.

There was a rustling on the other end of the line, and a new voice replaced the chief's. "Madousin, get the hell out of there. You aren't of age to fight a level four."

Dane reached down reluctantly for the throttle. The ash fall was growing thicker. Frowning, he peered out his windows. The smoke all but eliminated his view now. This thing was growing fast, and, from the looks of it, the hot zone was approaching at a rapid clip.

As he started to reverse, static flared on the radio. He thought he heard the word *help* but couldn't make out anything else.

"This is Dane Madousin. Didn't catch that last. Please repeat."

"Don't mess with me," came the voice from control. "I said to get out of there."

"No," Dane tried to explain. "I thought I heard something else. Is there anyone out there?"

More scratching and nothing clear.

Dane glanced at his radar. No sign of the promised backup planes. But something was sending off a signal, very faint and not very far off, behind him.

"Tell the chief I think there's someone—"

"Madousin, get back here now!" the fire chief boomed.

Dane switched off the radio. He eased *Gold Dust* into motion, backing toward the signal. As the smoke cleared enough to spot the ground, he searched for a break in the tree cover. Spaces meant water or a protection zone around a man-made structure. Whatever his radar had picked up, it was not natural, and no zone was going to be much help in the face of this fire.

He rifled through his memory, trying to remember if he had seen any structures on the map. No, there should not be any buildings here at all. Unless the map—

Then he saw it, coming out from this side of the blaze. Not a building but a straight strip designating a road. A rusty red land vehicle stuttered out of the smoke. No way was that contraption going to outrace the blaze. One change in the wind and the wheeled machine would be fodder for the flames.

Dane shifted his plane into motion, and it swept down in a sloping crescent. Squeezing into the narrow space between the tree trunks and the land vehicle, *Gold Dust* hovered beside the other machine. Dane motioned to the driver to pull over, but the haze was so thick he was not sure the frantic hand motions could be seen. Not until the land vehicle jolted to a halt.

Pulling ahead, Dane dropped the plane down onto the hard-packed earth. In the danger zone now. He felt a lurch of adrenaline as he slid on his oxygen mask then, with one fluid motion, shoved open the pilot's side door and leaped out, dropping six feet to the road's surface.

A booming roar shocked him to the ground, the sound of fire battering through timber. He dragged himself up into the stifling air and sought out the land vehicle. The driver had left his cab but seemed to be having trouble walking. His clothes were caked in soot, and he stumbled, his back hunched over, his chest lowered to his waist. *Smoke inhalation.*

Dane hurried forward, grabbed the man around the back, and hauled him toward the far side of the plane, one lurching step at a time. Hot air whipped strong in Dane's face, a reminder they were at the wind's mercy. Gone was the plane's shimmer of fresh paint, its golden color smeared with blown ash. Releasing his hold on the man in order to scale the side of the aircraft, Dane jerked open the door and leaped again to the road.

The man had slumped to the ground, his body on its side, curled in a tight ball. He struggled to sit up but collapsed back against the earth. Dane reached down to help, then somehow pushed, heaved, and shoved the weak body up toward the open space in the cockpit doorway.

A drooping arm caught in the strap of the oxygen mask, pulling the cover out of position. Acrid smoke invaded Dane's lungs. Gagging, he thrust the body into the passenger seat and slammed shut the door, then raced around the plane's nose, fingers tearing at his mask but only managing to tangle the strap. He gave up, needing his hands to climb into the pilot's seat.

Within seconds, the plane lifted off the ground. The

cockpit had filled with smoke, and Dane's eyes watered as he steered the aircraft out of the fog.

He tried to switch the radio back on to no avail. No response, not even static. The radar remained blank. Either it too was failing or the extra planes had never arrived.

Harsh coughing echoed from the man in the other seat. Soot coated his skin, making age and facial features hard to discern, but the pain was easy to read. Dane finally wrenched off his own mask and slipped it around the man's head.

Then he set the coordinates for the hospital on base and shifted into a higher gear. *Zhzhzh!* They were soaring. Way, way over the speed limit, but the hell with that. The passenger had slumped over, his head upside down at an odd angle against the door, and there was no telling if he was still breathing.

The outskirts of the city drifted into focus—rectangular shapes, straight walls, and pointed pyramids littering the horizon. Dane swerved to the left, hoping to avoid the traffic and the city flight patrol. He veered around the city's rim.

The sterile gray-green structures of the Alliance Air Force Base stretched out to the west. Dane ripped into military airspace without missing a beat, eased up on the power as he spotted the hospital landing pad, and touched down with a precision that would make any pilot cringe in envy. Even his father.

But there was no time to savor the moment. Figures rushed toward the plane. Coughing himself now, Dane wrapped his arms around the passenger's sooty chest and lowered the listless body into the outstretched arms of a medic.

He scrambled down to answer questions, but a heavy arm shoved him up against the side of the plane.

"Dane Madousin?" The harsh voice grated in his ear.

Dane coughed. "Y-yes."

Cold steel closed around his wrists. "You're under arrest."

Chapter Two
THE INVITATION

THE HATCH TO AERIN'S COMPARTMENT ON THE *Envoy* opened with a cold, sucking sound. Four weeks she had been on board this ship, and still she could not accustom herself to that sound. It seemed to scrape into the recesses of her brain.

She stiffened but remained seated on the narrow bench of the tight personal quarters. They could not quite be defined as a room since, aside from the bench and the mirror on the opposite wall, the compartment's only furniture consisted of the retractable bed which, had it been folded down, would have filled the entire six-by-four-foot space.

The rising hatch revealed the black boots, dark uniform, and gray head of the captain. He crossed swiftly under the low entryway without needing to duck. She knew better by now than to judge him by his small size. No slight personality could have run such a huge vessel and earned the respect of the massive crew. And he had done so. How he had done it, she did not know, but she had seen the way the men and women under his command watched his every move, leaping to obey, even when it meant halting a major voyage to answer a distress call from a broken trade ship.

Aerin still could not believe he had answered. She kept checking her shadow, waiting for the whip to fall or the deadbolt to slide into place, but she had been subjected to nothing other than an array of physical and mental tests upon the first week of her arrival. Still, this might be the time.

Goose bumps rose on her flesh.

The captain cracked a crooked grin and handed her a heavy, tightly sealed white box. "A package arrived for you from the Council."

Council? Her tongue remained flat on the bottom of her mouth as she set the box on the bench and ran her hands over the package's smooth surface to see if she could find an opening. Nothing, but then maybe she was doing something wrong.

The captain reached down and pulled a thin, black-handled knife from his boot.

She felt her pulse quicken and backed away, slamming her spine and shoulders against the wall.

He did not react except to turn the handle around until it faced her, then held it out in her direction.

An extended moment passed before she realized he wanted her to take the knife and use it to open the box. With darting quickness, she grabbed the weapon and held it secure.

The captain remained still, watching her.

With a single, agile slice, she split open the package. Out onto the bench tumbled a blue packet and black clothing: boots, slacks, socks, and a shirt with ebony buttons. Such fine fabric. She reached out a tentative finger, then drew back.

"Go ahead; it's yours," said the captain, retrieving the knife and returning it to his boot. "Standard-issue uniform. Means the Alliance has placed you in a school." He peered into the box at its remaining contents. "An academic one, judging by the thickness of those textbooks." One eyebrow lifted in curiosity as he handed her a sealed letter. "This came as well. Read it and see where you're headed."

Aerin obeyed, but the written words made little sense.

Prying her tongue off the base of her mouth, she forced herself to speak for the first time since boarding the giant vessel, not to tell him the name of the school listed in the letter, but to ask one of the hundreds of questions battering her mind. "What is the Alliance?"

The captain's eyes widened. He rocked back on the heels of his polished boots and for one panicked, heart-stopping moment, Aerin feared she had made a severe error. Then he chuckled, taking a seat on the edge of the bench, several feet away. She tensed at this nearness but forced herself to remain still. "Well, there's a hard question. Not sure I've ever had to answer it before, but then I don't often travel this far outside the boundary."

She waited, uncomfortable with his laughter.

"I suppose the simplest response is to say the Alliance is the largest government in the universe," he said, "composed of five central star systems. Delegates from every member planet run the government."

"Delegates?" she asked.

"Yeees." He scratched his head as if having trouble deciding how to explain. "The people on the planet pick someone to represent them. All those on the planet must have a say."

Imagine if all the people on Vizhan had a say in who their leaders were. Life would be very different then.

The captain went on, his curved fingers tapping restlessly on the muscle of his thigh. "Of course there are too many delegates to work quickly or smoothly, so there is also a Council made up of four respected leaders. The Council listens to the delegates and makes decisions."

"And what does this Council have to do with my attending school?" she asked.

"Education is the backbone of the Alliance. In fact, one of the council members is also the principal of Academy 7, the most prestigious school in the universe."

Aerin lifted her head, but the captain kept talking, the tapping of his boots now moving in sync with his restless fingers. "Every young citizen between the ages of sixteen and seventeen is given the A.E.E., Academy Entrance Exam. That's the test I gave you after you boarded this vessel. Not like any other exam you've taken, is it?"

"No." The word *test* had other meanings to her. It meant using the skills she had to survive. It did not refer to solving problems or running for a length of time. The questions she had struggled with the most on the A.E.E. were the opening ones. *Parents' names:* she had left her mother's blank. *Schools attended:* the captain had filled that in for her with the word *homeschooled,* though he could not have known he was partly correct.

"What are the scores used for?" she asked.

"To place you in an academy. There are schools all over the Alliance now, in addition to the original seven. Test scores place you in the one most likely to suit your skill level."

Aerin's mind whirled. A government that not only allowed everyone to learn but actually wanted them to? The idea sounded far-fetched, but the captain did not look like he was teasing.

His eyes were sober, staring at the dyed design on her gray headband. He had done that enough that she knew he recognized the mark of Vizhan. He could not know the story of her past, but between that mark and her ragged appearance, he must have some idea of what she had been through.

His gaze dropped to the clothes at her side. "I should leave you to try those on." But he did not move. Instead, he glanced toward the textbooks, then stretched his right hand and closed it in a fist. "You might want to begin to study. As I said, the Alliance funds the education of all its *citizens.*"

And then she understood what this man had done: thrown her a chance, a single chance at a future, in the form of a test she should never have been allowed to take. Could she do what he was implying? Pretend to be a citizen of a world she had never known existed? But what other choice was there? She had no one, and nowhere else to go. If this was her chance, she must take it.

Her chin lifted.

And he stood, unfurling his fist against the smooth surface of the wall. "You have a month to prepare before your arrival." He waited a moment, as if expecting her to say something, perhaps the name of the school for which she had been selected.

But Aerin was not yet ready to share.

The captain turned away, the hatch door sliding down behind him.

She remained seated for a minute, then moved to the wide glass hanging on the wall. The face she saw in the reflection was already a stranger. Her sun-bleached hair had darkened, its natural brown strands brushed clean and straight. Her once bronze skin had paled around her high cheekbones and pointed chin, and though her ragged dress revealed the sharp points of her shoulders, elbows, and ribs, already the meals on board had begun to fill in the flesh around her bones.

She looked back at the black shirt, slacks, and boots on the bench. What person would she be when she changed into them?

Slowly her fingers reached up to slide the gray headband off her forehead. Even as she gazed down at the dyed V on the front of the band, she could still feel its imprint. Could she truly slip out of her past so easily? Relinquish it with the tattered rags?

Then her eyes flitted to the folded letter on the bench. She picked it up and tucked it into the bottom corner of the mirror. Could she brush off her memories and the last six years for a future thick with the unknown? Nothing could be worse than what she knew already. She wanted nothing left to remind her of the fields, the platforms, and the lasers. She would scrub them all away like she had the dirt from her bare feet. When she was done, there would not be a single sign of where she was from. Except for the brand on her shoulder, dark bars showing now where her wide neckline dropped down.

Dane awoke to the harsh creak of cell bars sliding across one another. He rolled slowly over onto his back, the hard springs of the dusty cot digging into his spine. His muscles ached from the long night at the police station, and his mouth tasted like smoke.

He had dreamed of fire: white-hot flames licking his face and eyebrows, heat burning his chest, smoke dousing his nostrils and clotting his air passages. The same smell now filled his pores, his clothes, and the uncomfortable jail cell mattress.

"Guess it helps having friends in high places." A mocking voice propelled him up off the bed. Outside the doorway stood a sallow-faced guard, a wide smirk on his lips.

"What do you know about it?" Dane replied.

The man twined a hand around a bar and rattled the open door. "You're outta here," he said.

With deliberate slowness, Dane stood, rubbing his knuckles along the side of his face. Soot as dark as his hair smeared the backs of his tan fingers. "What's wrong? You guys can't afford the soap to clean me up?" he cracked, then slid past the guard, sidestepping a stain on the cement floor, and sidled down the hall.

The waiting room greeted him with a display of smug police photos and the scent of burned coffee. Between the row of empty chairs and the front desk stood a familiar figure: a slouched sixty-year-old man in greasy coveralls, hands buried in wide pockets. Dane smiled.

"I don't know," the overweight cop at the front desk was saying. "Mr.?"

"Pete," replied the figure, dismissing the need for a surname.

"It's against policy to release a juvenile to someone other than a parent or legal guardian." Beefy arms crossed over a bulging stomach, and the cop leaned back in his padded chair.

Dane opened his mouth to protest that he had known Pete all his life. The aged mechanic had taught him to fly, checked in on him when his father was gone. And had been there for Dane when things got tough. Really tough.

But Pete held up a hand, halting the protest before it began, then straightened and gave the cop a hard stare. "His father is not on planet, as you well know. He won't return from his mission for another six weeks. But by all means, wait. See how he reacts when he hears his son has been locked up without any formal charges."

"Without—?" Dane started to ask.

"Sit down and shut up," ordered Pete.

Dane sat.

The cop's face bloomed red, a double chin jutting forward. "All right, but this is the last time I make an exception. The man redirected his gaze at Dane. "You hear that, Madousin? Show up here again after your seventeenth birthday, and we won't cut you another break, no matter what your last name is."

Dane gritted his teeth but let Pete's firm grip guide him out through the grimy station doors before he could word a comeback. The heat outside assaulted him. He banged his thigh on a rusty railing and glared with annoyance around the Gray Zone. No one else stirred amid the cramped trio of buildings designated for both city and base use, and not a single aircraft rested on the empty gravel landing pad.

"*Gold Dust*?" Dane questioned, suddenly worried about his new plane.

"You know you've been fired, right?" Pete growled.

Dane shrugged. Firefighting was not exactly his dream job. He knew better than to dream.

But damn it! he thought. "I earned that plane."

"It's back in the hangar," said Pete. "You're walking home, and you're lucky the police didn't impound her."

"They had no right. You know I didn't deserve to be—"

"Oh, I know all right. I know I've seen you in that place too many times." Pete marched his charge through the gate in the barbed-wire fence that separated the Gray Zone from the rest of Chivalry Military Base.

"For what? Reckless endangerment?" Dane argued, without sparing a glance for the armed patrol members lining the fence. "Come on, there's no way they could make that stick, not when the plane belonged to me instead of the fire company."

"This isn't about the plane." Pete's grip clenched on Dane's shoulder as they headed down a narrow passage. The high walls of the Allied Air Force facility rose up on the left. On the right, a ball game stood frozen, its young players absorbed with watching the passersby. Pete ignored the stares. "You'd still be sitting in that cell if the man you saved hadn't been a retired colonel."

"Because most people who save lives are treated as criminals." Sarcasm filled Dane's voice.

"Most people don't fly into a hot zone after being ordered out of it."

"So what if I am a few days underage to fight a level four? I'm a better flyer than most of those guys."

"You didn't go into that fire to save someone's life," Pete said, "and you know it. Reckless endangerment is an apt term whether or not the charges were dropped. Stop trying to kill yourself, or one of these days you're going to succeed."

Maybe, Dane thought. There were worse things. Like living under his father's control.

An uneasy pause stalled the conversation.

Even at this early hour, the base was never silent. The shouts of personnel, whirr of running motors, and beeping of traffic signals filled the air. And the cement surface did little to absorb the sound or the flashing lights from the spinning security tower at the heart of the action. Dane had a flashback to the wilderness he had flown over the previous day and felt a sudden urge to escape. He pulled away.

"Wait." Pete let out a slow sigh, the muscles on his worn face easing as he dug a hand into his pocket and held out an envelope. "This came for you. The housekeeper gave it to me when I stopped by to tell her I was picking you up. There's a package that goes with it." The gold seal gleamed at Dane.

Without taking the envelope, he began to walk down the long slanted edge of the airstrip. The glaring sun formed visions of deep puddles floating on the wide diagonal runway, and a solid wall of wire fencing loomed in the foreground.

Pete came up behind him, pointing at the envelope. "You know what this is?"

"The letter with my A.E.E. scores," Dane said, stepping purposefully on a crack. "Only the Council cares enough about secrecy to use traditional post."

"You plan to open it?"

Again Dane's eyes flew to the security seal. He couldn't open it, couldn't let himself care. "No."

"Then you won't mind if I do?" The words were a request.

"It's not as if some test has anything to say about me."

Pete retrieved the envelope's contents. His head jolted back slightly as he began to read; then his shoulders relaxed and he handed Dane the letter. "If the test isn't worth anything, why put forth the effort to place well?"

The name of the school curled its way through Dane's mental defense system, and he had to struggle a moment to regain his shield of disdain. "Paul," he answered. "When he took the A.E.E. two years ago, he failed to earn a spot in Father's alma mater."

"Ah. And sibling rivalry is always a priority over pretending to be stupid?" Pete said.

Hell, yes. In Dane's entire life, his brother had never failed at anything, at least not in their father's eyes. Until the school's rejection. And even then, it had been the school that had taken on the blame. Not the golden son, following in their father's footsteps.

Dane tossed the letter to the ground and continued walking. "It's not as if I'll attend."

"What?" The mechanic came to a sudden halt.

"My father hates that school." Dane flung the truth at the older man. "You don't really think he'd let me go there." *Never in a millennium.*

Anger and confusion flashed across Pete's face, then disappeared, crushed beneath derision. "*Let* you? Like he *let* you join the fire company, or he *let* you earn a spot in the base holding cell? Since when do you do anything your father wants? He won't even be back here by the time school starts." Pete made a sharp gesture toward the fallen paper. "That is your future, kid. You'd better pick it up."

* * *

Dear Student,

Congratulations! You have placed among the top fifty students taking the Academy Entrance Exams and are, therefore, selected to join the first-year class of the most exclusive school of higher education in the universe, Academy 7. Your uniform, detail packet, and textbooks are enclosed in the accompanying package. Please be aware that your exam scores provide you only with entrance into the school. They do not ensure your ability to stay.

Sincerely,

Dr. Jane Livinski

Council Member & Principal, Academy 7

Dr. Livinski reread the unsigned invitation on her office desk. She paused, running a hand over the tight bun at the back of her head, and adjusted the wire rims of her glasses. Then with a brisk movement, she signed the form and pushed away the paper.

That was the last of them. Fifty invitations. Another full class of first-years.

Her hand closed tightly around the coffee mug to her right, and for a moment she held still, daring the heat to burn her palm. Steam rose up from the dark depths, then evaporated before reaching her face.

Fifty new students. Another class of cocky, naïve first-years who had never faced a challenge they could not meet. But some of them would face one here, half of them in fact. At least half.

Because that was how she wanted it. Her gaze flew back toward the final form letter. The word *Congratulations* seemed to stare at her. She would not have chosen to begin the letter that way. It set up false hope. As though the students had been invited to a party with frosted cake and colored streamers.

No, it was the last line Dr. Livinski preferred. The one that gave warning. She had been quite clear to the new secretary about that line. She just had not thought to tell him about the first one.

Too late now, though. She had signed half the forms without paying attention, and by the time she had read one, many were already in the general post. Nothing to do at that point but send out the final letters. It would not take the students long to learn that Academy 7 was no pastry confection.

With a thin smile, she straightened up in her hard oak chair, stretching. Her auburn tweed jacket strained against the movement, and she lapsed back into normal position, then focused her mind on the high stack of student files at the edge of the desk.

Her secretary had stared in wonder at that stack when he had learned he would have to scan all the data into the computer lab's high-security files. "Must be important," he had said.

"Score reports," Dr. Livinski had replied.

Not fascinating reading. She began the arduous task, first ignoring the names and sorting the stack from lowest to highest exam score. Then, starting with the file of the lowest-scoring student, she worked her way through the pile.

It was mind numbing what the Board of Education felt principals should know about new pupils: birth dates, family members, schools attended. As if any of those could tell her whether the students would succeed here, whether they would have the strength and stamina. And, far more important, the will.

The hours dragged on. By the time she reached the final two files, the room outside her office was dark. Her secretary had left more than an hour before, and the building was silent. She eyed the last two folders with a frown, then decided to tackle them both at once and be done.

She shuffled the files side by side, flipped open the front flaps, and dropped her gaze to read. Only then did her calm demeanor change. A hand tightened around her cold coffee mug, and for a second the room seemed to swim. How could this have happened? There, printed in bold ink, were the names Dane Madousin and Aerin Renning.

Chapter Three
ON HALLOWED GROUND

As Aerin stepped off the *Envoy* onto the planet of Academia, the sounds of Seventh City throbbed around her: small hovercraft zipping along the narrow, crooked streets; peddlers hawking blankets from crowded wooden stands; bells pealing from clock towers. The city vibrated with what seemed to be a rich blend of modern life and ancient tradition.

But Aerin's blood ran icy cold at the sight of the Wall. The captain had briefly mentioned it in his directions, but his description had been far from adequate. The Wall's slick face towered in the distance before her, rising up in a sweeping circle, blocking from her view the school she knew was at the barrier's center. And the surface of the Wall was black. The color of a shroud.

Suddenly, she could feel neither the invitation in her hand nor the strap of her bag over her shoulder. She could feel nothing. Except a rigid icicle shell settling over her body. Had she escaped the terror of slavery, risking her life and perhaps those of others, to walk right back into confinement?

She forced herself to move forward, refusing to look back at the *Envoy* as it departed into the sea green sky with its crew and captain. For almost eight weeks, she had lived in the quarters of the giant vessel, spending the latter four pouring through her textbooks and everything she could find on the Alliance. And now the *Envoy* was gone, taking with it the remnants of her father's ship. Another link with the past severed.

Ten city blocks faded beneath her feet as she approached the Wall. A hulking guard with a ragged beard stood at the base of two huge doors. "Invitation?" he demanded. Aerin released her tight grip on the crumpled paper.

"Path to your left," said the guard, pressing his weight to a door. Hinges creaked, and a narrow crack formed, large enough for a single human to slip through. Somehow Aerin did so. With the closing boom, her inner walls hardened, stronger than any structure in metal.

No one met her on the other side, only a strange, surreal quiet.

A thin path of cracked cement swept forward into the enclosed circle, then split in a sharp V. Her gaze followed the right fork to a massive building made not of space-age metal but crumbling stone. The high arch over the entrance sagged above slanted steps, and Aerin could just make out the words GREAT HALL on a rusted sign.

Behind the hall, a structure unlike anything she had ever seen soared into the air. Its slender stem, of the same black material as the Wall, stretched thousands of feet above even that high circle. At the top of the stem balanced a diamond-shaped formation, its black outline shot through with a white center. At the diamond's base, a curling black tube wound its way out in a wide circle, then spiraled down in tighter and tighter loops for perhaps a thousand feet. And the entire structure moved, turning counterclockwise in steady rotation.

Aerin dragged her stare away, seeking solace from the dizzying movement. She found none between the hall and herself, nothing but the path and a flat green lawn. Relentless open space, like the work fields on Vizhan. A chill shuddered her torso.

But the guard had said to go left. Her feet turned quickly down the fork, crossed another path, and hurried on. She passed by a sunken brick building, her stomach slightly rumbling as she noted rows of empty cafeteria tables through smudged glass windows.

It was the garden, however, that made her slow her steps. Thick overgrown greenery of every shade embraced her: long, drooping ferns sprouting up from the ground; heart-shaped leaves stretching from bushes and hedges; soft, mossy fingers draping down from hanging tree limbs. Here among the foliage, she was hidden. If someone approached along the path, she could duck behind the green curtain and peer through the branches.

She lifted the palm of one hand to a silky red petal and breathed in the deep scent of pollen. Sweet. And somehow calming, despite her walled surroundings. For the first time since entering the school grounds, she allowed herself to feel.

And to think. Why were the grounds so quiet? Surely there should be others present. But there was no sign of anyone. She continued forward, propelled now by curiosity.

Another building emerged from the foliage, this one, like the hall, showing the signs of age. Three stories high, it featured a brick facade overgrown with ivy. Two wings stretched east and west, and a front door stood open, propped with a heavy block.

The sound of an argument drifted out the opening and sliced through the stillness. "I can't understand you, Yvonne," said a cool, mature woman's voice. "You should feel no compulsion to stay with only two first-years left to sign in."

"And I thought you wanted me to take on more responsibility, Mother," mocked a sharp female voice.

"Don't quote my words as a weapon. I have the quality of your position in mind. Leadership is noticed."

"I doubt I'll need the extra credit," replied the daughter. "After all those wretched private lessons you made me take, I'm bound to be among the top students."

"I certainly hope you won't be *among* them. You are an

Entera. Nothing less than the best will be sufficient. Our planet bears our family name, and, as a member, you represent all of us."

"Just because every Entera for the past three hundred years has been an Academy 7 wing monitor does not mean I should," the girl complained. "I'd rather lead the social committee."

"Well you can't associate with everyone, now, can you?"

Aerin crept up the stoop, hoping she had reached the right place. Through the open doorway, she could make out the corner of a lobby. A dim lamp perched on the edge of a counter, and a ratty brown couch stretched out behind a low footstool. Elsewhere in the room, still out of sight, the quarrel flared on.

"Honestly, Yvonne," continued the woman, "the radio announced the entrance into local airspace to all and sundry, you know. *Why* are you still there?"

"Really, Mother"—sarcasm ripped through the daughter's voice—"are you advising me to abandon my duties because some criminal is about to arrive on school grounds?"

The term *criminal* sent a chill through Aerin's spine. Were they talking about her? Her mind rifled through the laws she had broken in the past two months, first by fleeing Vizhan and now by attempting to pass herself off as an Allied citizen. Her thoughts flashed back to the protective shelter of the gardens, but she could not flee now, not without notice. She had entered the lobby.

An exotic young woman about Aerin's age sat perched, one leg crossed over the other, on the corner of a table. Olive-brown skin gleamed at her throat where she had failed to secure the top two buttons of her uniform, and the girl's black eyes glittered at a shimmering image cast upon the wall. Her voice dropped its mocking tone. "Don't you think it would better if my first conversation with him was here?" She emphasized the last two words. *"In private."*

The image, that of an elegant woman in a sculpted white hat, relinquished a patronizing smile. "Oh, darling," she said, fingering a long necklace of opaque pearls, "how naïve you are." The fingers allowed the pearls to fall. "Young men with his quality of background don't *have* privacy. If you wait until he arrives here, he'll already have an entourage. You'd best make sure you're leading it."

The daughter's black eyes wavered, then shot toward the door. And landed for the first time on Aerin. An appalled expression flashed across Yvonne's face as she snapped shut the silver device in her hand. Instantly the image of the mother evaporated. *A personal transmitter,* Aerin realized as she stared at the silver object that had been clearly listed in the student handbook as not allowed on campus.

Yvonne buried the communication device into her pocket and whipped a long swath of black hair over her shoulder. "You would arrive now," she said, her glare outlawing any mention of the banned transmitter.

Aerin felt a strange heat rise to her cheeks. She of all

people was not about to turn someone in for breaking the rules.

"Last name?" Yvonne picked up a clipboard.

Aerin's fingers dug sharply into the splintered door frame. What if someone had found out where she was from? Would she be sent back? Or punished? She could give a false name, but a lie would draw instant attention. Besides, she knew her real name had been on the entrance exam. The captain must have found a way for the records to list her as an Allied citizen, as long as no one looked too hard. "Renning," she finally said, telling the truth.

The girl flipped a page. "Your schedule, extra uniforms, and group designation should be in your room. Those of us in the first-year class are split into two groups because of the higher number of students. All three classes stay here: seniors on the ground floor, juniors second, first-years at the top; girls in the west wing, guys in the east. Hallways are open to anyone. Curfew is at ten o'clock." She held out an envelope.

Aerin had to relinquish her grip on the door frame in order to take the sealed paper.

"Your room is 307," continued Yvonne. "The entry code is inside the envelope. Security is high priority around here." She uncrossed her legs and stood up. "No swapping rooms. We all have the same cramped space." A faint smile flashed. "I'm sure you can find your way."

And with that she swept around the table's edge and out the door, disappearing in a rush of perfume. The cloying scent and departing footsteps faded until once again Aerin was alone. She slowly crossed the room, then wound her way up the tight staircase to the third floor, and entered a stark hallway spotted with rows of closed doors. Nothing else moved in the hall, not a voice or a breeze or a scrap of paper. Her throat constricted, and she had an image of herself walking unknowingly to execution.

There. She stopped at a door identical to the others except for the number 307 etched in the chipped paint. With trembling fingers, she opened the envelope in her hand and shook out a slick piece of paper. The numbers written on it blurred before her, but she blinked to clear her vision and forced her hand not to shake as she punched the code into the keypad. The door screeched its way open.

And she saw *her room.* The real meaning of the words became clear only as Aerin stepped inside. Cramped? It was sheer luxury. A bed stretched along the wall, clean white blankets covering the mattress. Between the headboard and the far wall were a wooden desk and matching chair, not to mention a computer and a small stack of notebooks. To her right stood an open closet, a shelf with a built-in basin, and a water spigot.

What she would have given for water in the crowded slave sheds on Vizhan!

A string with a handle dangled from the ceiling, the word *pull* etched on the handle's end. She obeyed.

And her heart stopped. For the beige curtain on the far

wall had lifted to reveal a window. A window! Eight feet wide. Her bag of heavy textbooks slipped from her shoulder to the floor. She stumbled forward, lifted the window, and leaned out into the welcoming arms of a giant maple tree.

Fresh air swept her face as she took in the view. The overgrown garden stretched beneath her, a glint of ivory sparkling at its tangled center. She let herself breathe, then slowly lifted her gaze, a single thought marring her ecstasy. *Where was everyone?*

Dane saw the crowd from the air. Black uniforms nibbled at the edge of the small Academy 7 landing pad at the school's southeastern rim, just inside the protective wall. A lot of good that protection would do him. He had a sudden desire to punch in new coordinates and redirect *Gold Dust* in the opposite direction.

Why had he let Pete con him into this? The old mechanic knew him too well, knew things Dane did not want to admit even to himself. And knew exactly how to push Dane's buttons. Now it was too late to turn back. Especially with all the pairs of gawking eyes watching.

Not that the crowd was a surprise, not really. After a month of being flogged in the Allied tabloids, he supposed a low-key entrance onto the grounds would have been too much to ask, even at the school boasting the most intelligent youth in the universe.

Refueling his determination, he pointed the plane's nose

toward the tarmac and swept in for his signature landing. Fast. Clean. And right into the assigned parking slot.

Wheels touched the earth, and he glanced out the window. Perhaps a hundred bodies began their approach, all wearing the same black garb. No teachers then. Well, that was something.

Giving himself one last moment of peace, he turned off the power and smoothed a hand over the rectangular edge of the steering equipment. "Guess this is it, *Gold Dust*. You're off-limits during term." Flight courses were restricted to upperclassmen. Dane breathed in the scent of newly cleaned leather and closed his eyes, imagining himself once more skimming through empty space.

Thudding boots disrupted the quiet as bodies formed a semicircle around the pilot's side of the plane. He considered exiting the other side, then discarded the idea.

Squeezing the door handle, he stepped out into a small space at the center of the writhing swarm. Murmurs, gasps, and giggles clashed in the air. Students jostled one another, pushing with knees and elbows to get a better view, pressing inward. Dane felt a familiar wave of annoyance simmer in his stomach. *Just ignore them. It's not like I haven't had enough practice.*

A slender young woman with olive-brown skin detached herself from the swarm and came forward. She gave those behind her a quelling glare, then turned an artificial smile in his direction. "I'm Yvonne," she said, her perfume assaulting his nostrils as she held out an envelope. "I brought your room code. Can I help you find your way?"

"That's really not necessary." He snatched the envelope from her green-painted nails and stepped free of the perfume. Her shoulders stiffened. She sent him a haughty look as she rejoined the ranks of the other students.

Dane gave an inward shrug. He had neither the time nor the desire for a fling. Girls always wanted to get too close, to know too much. Especially pretty ones. He flipped open the outside compartment on the plane and removed two luggage bags.

The crowd began to hum, bodies shifting and pressing against one another. By the time he had heaved the bags into his grip, a narrow opening had formed. He walked through it, conscious of the gap closing behind him. Then, free of the tangle, he set off across the tarmac, heading north.

A male shout cut him off, ramming its way forward from behind the crowd. "Hey, Madousin! Landing speed is fifteen miles per hour. You break it again, you won't even make it to the end of term."

The crowd's laughter welled up, broken by an instant hush as Dane dropped his bags and turned. With deliberate slowness, he ran his eyes over the group, daring each member to meet his gaze. *You want to stare? Fine. But intimidation? I don't play that game.* One by one the faces looked down.

His hands reached again for the bags, and he walked away. *As if there's even a chance I'll make it to end of term,* he thought wryly. He had two and a half weeks until his father yanked him. At the most.

Dr. Livinski coughed as she entered the auditorium of the Great Hall. Thank goodness opening ceremony required only a podium at the front of the room. The lone janitor had already wiped down the slatted floor and wooden benches, but dust still clung to the air; Dr. Livinski dreaded what would happen once someone moved the stage's heavy maroon curtain. This, however, was not the time to bemoan the sad state of the cleaning budget.

She had other priorities.

By now the hall outside should be bursting with students. Two of which she had an unusual interest to see.

Seating herself in the front corner of the room, she tucked her feet under the sharp edge of the chair and smoothed her straight beige skirt over her legs, then nodded consent for the doors to be opened.

The third-years entered first, calm and controlled, with heads held high. They walked not in a straight line but with a sense of purpose, each to his or her own place, without hesitation or hurry. They were seated within moments. Dr. Livinski smiled at the familiar faces, those of young men and women almost ready to take on active roles in the Alliance.

The same could not be said for the second-years, who arrived in a semblance of a brigade with too many captains and several loose cannons. One young woman tried to tell each person where to sit while a taller male classmate argued with her. Both scowled at a student wearing a pop-up watch and a pair of fluorescent AV goggles. A handful of stragglers burst in late, and Dr. Livinski found herself wondering which members of the class would buckle down to handle the advanced work of the second year and which ones she would have to send home with a letter of regret.

The disorder of the juniors, however, was nothing next to that of the first-years. The new pupils arrived in an awkward mass of gangly arms and legs, heads turning this way and that, voices raised in excitement. Instead of seating themselves quickly in the empty benches at the front of the room, they chose to scramble over one another in attempts to find seats farther back. Then, having reached the empty spots, they changed their minds, shuffling here and there and switching positions.

With no hope of recognizing any of the new students amid the turmoil, Dr. Livinski resigned herself to a longer wait and made her way briskly to the podium.

The chaos subsided as she began to speak, her deep voice powering its way to the back of the room. "This is the five thousand twenty-first year of Academy 7." She let the words hang in the air. "To participate in this school is not a privilege. It is a challenge requiring hard work and commitment, nothing less. If you succeed in graduating, you will mark yourselves as the future of the Alliance."

A change swept over her listeners. Sprawled legs crept

inward. The goggles vanished under a bench, and gazes zeroed in where they belonged.

She launched into the climax of the speech. "Members of the first-year class, in the rare chance that you have not heard, I must make one fact quite clear. Fifty first-years are chosen to join Academy 7 each year, but the greatest number of slots open for the junior class is twenty-five. And let me assure you, that number is by no means guaranteed. Whether or not you return will be determined entirely by me."

A heavy quiet descended, the weight of her words settling down over the new pupils. She waited, letting the moment stretch and expand until the silence itself became part of the challenge. Then she added, "I shall now introduce each one of you. Please stand when I call your name."

The students did as they were told. Neither of the two Dr. Livinski wanted to see did anything exceptional. Aerin popped up then rapidly down as if trying to disappear, and Dane, who could not help but garner attention, stood and sat while holding his gaze locked on the wall, as though he hoped his curious audience might lose interest if he ignored them. Dr. Livinski severely doubted the offspring of Gregory Madousin or Antony Renning had any chance of blending in.

Chapter Four
CLOSE ENCOUNTERS

ACADEMIA'S SUN HAD BARELY CLEARED THE HORIZON when Dane stumbled up the stairs for his first class. The world was still a blur, and he nearly wrenched his ankle on the Great Hall's uneven steps before reaching the third floor. He frowned at the tightly crammed classroom and rows of already-seated students, checked the timepiece on his wrist—not late—and wove through the old-fashioned desks to an empty chair.

It rocked forward, trying to spit him back out. He scowled at the bent chair leg and scanned the room for another vacant seat. Nothing remained except a broken bench propped against a bare wall. Resigning himself to staying put, he dropped his forehead to his desk and tried to clear the haze from his mind. Whoever had scheduled debate for this early in the morning deserved a commute through an asteroid belt.

"I am Mr. Xioxang," a man's deep voice cut through the haze. Dane lifted his head to find gold eyes tearing into his skull. Red teacher's robes draped the man's towering frame, and a slick hood outlined the sharpness of his face. In his left hand, he held a pen and a dark notebook. "Who can tell me why the Alliance is the greatest nation in the universe?"

Dane looked away. This was why he hated school. It was full of opinions presented as fact. Around him a mass of hands sprang into the air. *Eager fledglings anxious to impress the hawk.*

Ignoring the hands, Xioxang swept forward. His curved fingers landed with a sharp rap on the desk of a girl filing her painted-green fingernails. She dropped the file and shot the teacher an offended look. "What?"

Dane recognized her from the day before, Sean or Dawn or something like that.

The teacher frowned. "Need I repeat the question, Miss Entera?"

She gave an unsubtle glance in Dane's direction, as if checking to make sure he was listening, then straightened her shoulders. "The reason the Alliance is great is because of the Manifest." *Yvonne:* that was her name.

"Why the Manifest?" the teacher probed. "How can a document make a nation great?"

It can't, Dane thought. *That's why your initial question is flawed.*

Yvonne pursed her gloss-covered lips. "It isn't the document itself, but the mission stated on it."

"What mission?" Xioxang drew closer.

She tossed her black hair over her shoulder. "The mission to create peace and stability by bringing every planet into the Alliance."

He groaned inwardly. *The Manifest doesn't say that. The mission is to unify all the planets, not absorb them.*

Mouth curved downward, the teacher made a sharp mark in his notebook, then slapped his palm on the abandoned nail file and snapped it in half.

Yvonne stiffened and opened her mouth as though to protest.

But the teacher had already swept away. He crossed to the back of the room and confronted a plain, skinny girl hiding behind a curtain of straight brown hair and a history text. "How?" demanded Xioxang. "How does the Alliance intend to spread lasting peace?"

Her response was soft but surprisingly quick. "Through equal rights and fair government."

Dane frowned. Not that he disliked the Manifest's ideals, but they were *ideals.* He couldn't have listed the number of times the Council had sidestepped them in favor of growth.

"Plagiarism is not worth any points in this classroom."

Xioxang lifted his pen to make another mark in his notebook.

But the girl lowered her text. "Then I disagree with the author's opinion, sir."

The pen froze. "How?"

She tucked her hair behind an ear. Dark eyes looked out of her solemn face into his penetrating stare. "If . . . if the Alliance believes in equal rights, why does it allow slavery to occur on X-level planets?"

Now there was a question.

The teacher once again lifted his pen. "That's a detail that would fit better in a later discussion."

"I doubt the slaves on those planets see it as a detail," she blurted, her voice growing louder.

"The Alliance cannot impose its moral code on a planet that is not a member," said Xioxang.

Right. Like that never happened.

The loose folds of the girl's uniform shifted over her thin torso, and her skin took on a rusty red shade. "The Alliance seems to have done so with any number of planets throughout its history." She gestured at her lowered textbook.

Dane was not tired now. His mind fastened on the argument.

Instead of admitting defeat, the teacher changed his tactic. "X-level planets are so labeled because their leaders allow inhumane treatment. By refusing those planets trade with the Alliance, the Council hopes to enforce change."

In Dane's opinion, it was the most reasonable argument the teacher had made thus far, but fury overtook the girl's face and posture. She leaned forward, catlike, elbows bent and palms flat on her desktop. As if she might launch out of her seat and attack the swirling robes of her opponent. Her chin jutted out, and sharp cheekbones underlined the anger seething in brown irises. For several moments, her tongue stalled, then words spilled out in a rush. "That kind of *hope* is worthless when the price is the lives of thousands of young children!"

Xioxang took a step back from the flames of her anger. Then a strange smile appeared on his thin lips.

Dane knew that smile. It was the one his father wore when he foresaw triumph. Unwilling to let the bastard win, Dane threw himself onto the pyre. "Sir, doesn't it seem wrong that our military has attacked Wyan-Ot when far greater crimes occur on X-level planets?"

A murmur traveled throughout the room, and something snapped from the direction of Yvonne's desk, probably another nail file.

Surprise flitted across the teacher's face before fading behind a measured response. "The military has not attacked Wyan-Ot, Mr. Madousin, as I'm sure you know. A small force has gone in to protect the planet from the Trade Union that had infiltrated their government."

"I suspect the three hundred Wyan-Ot soldiers who died in the conflict viewed it as an attack. And you just highlighted her question." Dane nodded toward the angry girl. "If the Alliance went in to protect the Wyannese, why doesn't it go in to protect the thousands of victims on X-level planets?"

There was no answer. The argument stalled, each participant holding still with gritted teeth.

Until the bell rang.

Xioxang strode to the front of the room, then turned abruptly, his gaze sweeping over the rest of the class. "What do you think?" he said. "Is Mr. Madousin right? Is she?" His forefinger pointed at the girl. "Am I?"

Silence stretched throughout the rows.

"Well, you'd better decide." The teacher snapped his notebook shut. "Because you won't pass this class by quoting a text, even the required one. And you won't pass by quoting me. I expect everyone here to have an opinion and to support it with a strong defense. Whether we're talking about Wyan-Ot. Or X-level planets." He paused. "Class dismissed."

Dane's thoughts reeled. Had he just been complimented? He stood up, wanting to speak to the girl with the vivid temper.

But she had fled the scene.

Her name, Dane soon learned, was Aerin Renning, and though she was nothing outstanding to look at, she had a mind like an Ephesian slicer. During science she rattled off the structure of an H_2O replicator; and in Universal

Literature, she was the only student to translate the ancient poem, "Migracion Humana."

Still, with the lure of food less than an hour away, Dane might have lost interest in her. If the events in technology class had not rendered that impossible.

The tech lab was in the basement. And based on the semi-crumbling state of the other classrooms, Dane would not have been surprised to wade through a swath of cobwebs on his way through the door. Clearly the government's decade of slashing the general fund in favor of defense spending had taken its toll on even the most famous school in the Alliance.

But the real condition of the room surprised him. Silver walls glimmered with data strips. Glassy panels covered the ceiling. Rows of cushioned, swivel chairs lined the tables: thirty chairs, one for each of the thirty state-of-the-art computers. *Ravens.* Dane recognized them. The tech lab must be supported by the Council.

A plump man in striped green robes gestured for the students to take their seats. His bushy beard flared out from his chin, and blue eyes sparkled above a crooked nose. Judging by his smile, he rather enjoyed the students' stunned reaction to the lab.

Dane noticed Aerin enter the room, take a few halting steps, then sink down, her attention riveted on the shining black machine before her. He slid into the chair beside hers.

"Welcome to the Academy 7 tech lab," said the robed man,

stuffing his hands into large pockets and rocking back on his heels. "I'm Mr. Zaniels, and this is my domain." He stuck out his chin in a smooth circle. "The database you can access from this room—and this room only—is the second largest in the Alliance. Your room code will serve as your password and will give you access to any data that might help with your schoolwork."

You mean the code will restrict us from anything we aren't allowed to see. Dane had heard about the Academy 7 database. There were supposed to be high-security files on every student ever to pass through the school: leaders, heroes, and criminals alike. Not even the military had control over those files.

Zaniels went on, "If you haven't seen this type of computer before, don't worry. Each of you is seated at a Raven ZL. The Raven has yet to hit the open market and works a little differently from other machines. Your challenge today is to be the first to retrieve the file titled"—he paused for emphasis—"Academy 7 Code of Conduct."

A chorus of groans greeted the name. "If you get stuck and are not sure what to do," continued Zaniels, "try something. Begin."

Dane glanced at the blank screen before him. He failed to see how winning would prove anything other than that he owned a Raven back on base. At his side, Aerin was running her hands along the edges of her machine. She tugged a strand of mousy brown hair between her teeth, then let her fingers hover over the keyboard. "Something wrong?" he asked her.

She pulled the strand from her mouth and eyed him warily. "We're supposed to figure it out for ourselves," she whispered.

Dane shrugged and lowered his voice conspiratorially as he leaned toward her. "Technically, Zaniels didn't say we couldn't help each other."

She pulled away, maintaining her distance, but her eyes flitted toward the other screens lighting up around the room. She bit her lip, then jerked her head in a quick nod. "Where is the power switch?"

He blinked. Sure there were differences between the Raven and other models, but this was not one of them. "It's already on. Just type in 'Alliance' for the entry code." He reached for her keyboard, but she beat him to it, her head whipping around and her fingers flying over the keys. She did not thank him.

Incensed at the sudden brush-off, Dane punched the entry code into his own machine. He typed in his password, skipped over an introduction that would have taken time to download, and zapped away a bothersome graphic. Within seconds, he was in the database, scanning an endless list of files. Unbelievable. There must be twice as much data here as on base.

There it was: the file's name. A message popped up listing the download time for clearing security as three minutes. He pushed his seat back and glanced at Aerin's computer.

The words *Code of Conduct* glowed in brilliant purple letters at the center of her screen. His mouth dropped.

Something resembling a smile twitched across her face, making it not quite so plain. She stretched a skinny arm over his keyboard and hit the Restart button.

Anger replaced shock. "What do you think you're—" he started to protest.

"Freeze it," she interrupted.

"What?"

"Just shut up and watch." Both her hands now usurped his keyboard. A few steps later and he was staring at the bright purple words blinking on his screen. Neither he nor she had entered his password.

Understanding scaled the inside of his chest. She had bypassed the entire security system.

And shown him how to do it.

Chapter Five
COMBAT

AERIN TRIED TO BLOCK OUT THE DEAFENING NOISE OF the cafeteria: utensils banging onto plates, plates onto trays, trays onto tables. Chairs scraped across floor tiles. Machines beeped at the entrance. And over it all came the jarring clash of a hundred voices talking about the first morning's classes.

She wanted out. Needed out.

But if she left, someone might notice. Instead, she retreated inside her head, bringing up the vision of the Code of Conduct, its list of three rules spinning on the backs of her eyelids. *Question. Commit. Strive.* She clung to the words. For six years her only code had been survival.

Here survival was different, the pitfalls invisible to the naked eye, obscured by the unknown. She had been on edge all morning, certain she would make a mistake.

"You know you made a fool of yourself today." A sharp voice confirmed her own fears. Painted-green fingernails brushed against the side of Aerin's tray, and an olive-brown hand propped itself on the table's edge. Yvonne leaned forward, balancing a salad plate on her left palm. "You can't possibly not know who he is," she said, biting into a hot chili pepper, then waving her hand as if to cool the taste.

Who who *is?* Aerin chose not to respond. One lesson she had learned on Vizhan was never to confirm another's accusation.

"You really don't, do you?" Yvonne's voice glinted with astonishment. Bending across the table, she whispered the name, "Dane Madousin," then pulled back, searching for some type of reaction.

None came. Aerin scrambled through her mental database, but the name meant nothing.

The girl gestured toward a young man lifting a gooey pastry from the dessert table. His sleeves were pushed up past his elbows, a white scar on his lower arm marring the brownness of his tan. Pale shadows traced the slight hollows of his cheeks and the rim of his jaw. His black hair curled halfway down his neck, and Aerin recognized the way he surveyed the room, his eyes searching without appearing to do so.

It was the boy from the tech lab, the one who had offered to help, then given her a strange look when she had asked how to start the machine. As if he knew there was something wrong. That she did not belong.

"He's the son of General Madousin." Yvonne's words came slowly, with heavy emphasis. "The Council member. And the head of the Allied military."

An ominous twinge pricked Aerin's stomach.

Yvonne went on, "During debate you criticized the Alliance for not saving some slaves or something, and he actually argued on your side."

Aerin's spoon tightened in her hand. The events from debate came flooding back. She had not meant to argue with the teacher, but he had rejected her first answer. And she could not afford to fail. He had made her so angry, hedging around her question, then dismissing all those people on X-level planets, all those victims, as if they were nothing. And then it had turned out the teacher was only testing her to see if she would stand up for her views. Well, she had. Precious little good it would do the people she had left behind.

Yvonne was still talking about Dane. "He even pretended to criticize the Wyan-Ot mission when everyone knows his father is in charge of it."

"Pretended?" The question slipped. Aerin vaguely remembered someone joining in her side of the argument, but by then she had been too upset to pay heed.

"Of course. You didn't think he was serious, did you?"

Aerin blinked, her cheeks flaming. He had been making fun of her then, perhaps all morning.

Yvonne lifted a hand to wave at a group of girls across the room, then shifted her plate and stood erect. "I just thought you should know." Her hips swayed as she walked away, and the backs of the green-painted fingernails on her right hand grazed against the arm of the young man she had been discussing.

Aerin cringed and stared down at her bowl. The cheese had congealed at the top of her soup, and the smell of garlic now turned her stomach. All month she had spent studying, but it had taken her less than a day to betray her own ignorance and become a target.

"Mind if I sit?"

She looked up.

Into the deep brown eyes of Dane Madousin.

"I was just leaving." She lurched to her feet but banged the table with her knee. Her tray jolted, and the milk glass tumbled sideways, spraying liquid all over the front of his uniform.

He stood there, frozen, his tray still in his hands, milk dripping down the black folds of his shirt and pants.

"Oh, I'm sorry," she gasped, then cursed herself. Why apologize when he had destroyed her entire morning? Flushed, she brushed past him, trying to ignore the burning stares of the other students. *Run! Get away!* her head screamed, but she made herself walk calmly. Somehow she dumped her tray onto the conveyer belt and strode through the swinging doors before breaking into a sprint.

Her feet pounded across the path. She burst through the outer fringe of the garden and continued on, deeper and deeper into the tangled core. At first she was just running, heeding neither where she was going nor the scratching branches. Then a small trickle of blood oozed into her eye and brought her to a stop.

She wiped a finger across the scrape, decided it was nothing serious, and moved on at a slower pace, pausing now to avoid raised roots and low-hanging limbs. A flash of white glinted through the trees, and for a moment she thought she might have circled back to the path, but as she listened, a sustained whisper reached her ears.

A chill slid along her neck. Another ten steps and she found herself standing on the edge of a white paved circle, ten feet wide. At the circle's center rose a plume of clear water, arcing up and outward, then tumbling in a fine spray.

The fountain acted as a trigger, releasing tension. Aerin's feet gave out from under her, and her body slumped to the ground just beyond the water's reach. She pulled her knees close to her chest and dropped her head.

Was this what she had become? A coward hiding within an even tighter circle than the Wall. She could not, *could not* live like this. And what was she running from? The rude behavior of one young man?

Nothing at the school truly frightened her. It was not this place, but the thought of it as being temporary. Of being sent back.

She closed her eyes and tried to force away the images of the beatings she had seen given to captured runaways. The slow, painful deaths on display for other slaves who might consider the same course of action. The blood. And the screams.

Yet she had chosen to run that risk. And she was not about to let one small mistake, or one person, interfere with her chance at a future.

Rising to her feet, Aerin brushed herself off. She would be a fool to think she could flip some switch and change the natural course of her feelings, but she would have to try. Facing down one challenge at a time. Beginning with Dane Madousin.

Dane turned out to be a greater challenge then Aerin had anticipated. The afternoon instructor, Miss Maya, who was in charge of physical fitness and combat training, ran all the first-years through a rigorous set of fitness tests at the south end of the lawn. Tests of speed, strength, and agility: running at a short distance, running at a long one, throwing weights, climbing nets, and jumping pits. Competitions for the most pull-ups in five minutes, the most sit-ups in ten. Timed rope climbs and an obstacle course.

Without exception, Aerin came second in every single test—right behind Dane. By midafternoon break, she no longer cared about conquering her fears. She just wanted to thrash him at something.

"Enough," Miss Maya called, clapping her hands and blowing on a silver whistle. "Huddle up." The teacher's youthful face and petite body made her look almost as young as the students, but her tight fitness suit revealed the toned muscles of a trained fighter. No one disobeyed her orders.

"All right," she said, "you have all seen enough to gauge the strengths and weaknesses of your classmates. Find a combat partner with a similar build and fitness level."

The huddle splintered, and Aerin tried to back away from the throng, but a tight grip clamped down on her shoulder. "Your partner is right here, Miss Renning." The teacher steered her in front of Dane.

He cocked a black eyebrow and held out a hand for Aerin to shake.

She declined, then frowned at the grin that spread across the width of his face. He must think he could easily defeat her.

Within minutes the class had split into pairs. Again Miss Maya blew her whistle. "The person you are standing across from may or may not be your partner at the close of today. We'll start with some basic challenges, and I will reshuffle you as you work. Your cohort at day's end *will* be your partner for the rest of term.

"This is *physical* combat," she continued. "You may use only your body and your environment. Spread out, ladies and gentlemen, and try to topple your partner to the ground.

"Without causing serious injury," she added belatedly.

Aerin felt nerves zip like static over her skin as she followed Dane to the outer edge of the group. *It's only a training session,* she reminded herself.

They faced off, his slender frame a mere four feet from hers. His hands rested at his sides; his shoulders slumped, relaxed.

But she had learned too much in the fitness tests to underestimate him.

Moving to the left, Aerin tried to feel the ground beneath her feet. The slick grass nullified the traction on her boots, and she longed to undo the laces and slip free the leather weights.

Her opponent, however, moved with ease, also circling left. She staggered her steps to see if he would adjust. He did. In his own time, without shuffling or losing flow. "I've been meaning to talk to you," he said, breaking the silence between them.

Trying to break my concentration. She switched direction, wanting to see him react.

His face remained calm as he shifted the other way, keeping his center squarely across from hers, not letting her deter him from talking. "About what you did in the lab."

Without warning, he spun in a quick turn, aiming a kick at her side. She stepped close to lessen his power and thrust his leg away with her hands. He smiled, leaping back out of reach. "In Zaniels's class," he continued, "that was something: the way you avoided the password. I've never seen anyone break through security like that."

Horror trickled down her shoulders like sweat. She had

thought of sidestepping the password as only a shortcut, not as breaking the rules. Was he threatening to turn her in?

Instead of gauging her reaction, his eyes watched her body, their depths flashing from dark to light as he circled into the sun's path. When he did meet her gaze, they held only a strange look of curiosity. "I don't suppose you'd like to share where you learned that trick?"

She whirled left, moving in for a hit.

He blocked with his right arm. "Guess not." His mouth twitched with humor.

What was this? His way of entertaining himself? She backed off, forcing him to make the next move.

It came once again without setup. He stepped in for a sideways blow to her chest. This time she countered, curving around and jabbing her elbow toward his abdomen. He danced away.

But she had learned what she needed to know. All his moves were predictable: blocks, hits, kicks—all things she had learned from her father when she was young. Before Vizhan. Before she'd had to fight for every meal and learned that creative violence was the only defense against starvation.

Once again she waited for Dane to attack. He took his time, choosing instead to waste his breath with more speech. "You had a point this morning, in debate."

Hadn't he derived enough pleasure from that episode

without using it here? Aerin reined in her temper. *He's trying to goad you into moving first,* she told herself.

Then it came. A quick rotation and a kick toward her hip.

She dropped low to the ground, used her right foot as a pivot, and swung her left leg under his feet. To his credit, he reacted with speed, jumping over the leg. But she had him anyway. His jump was all defense with no counter.

He was barely out of the air when she hooked his knee with the inside of her elbow and pulled forward. Hard. Down he fell. His leg came out from under him, and his back hit the ground with a solid thud.

Aerin waited, crouched at his side until she saw the first rise and fall of his chest. The maddening smile was gone, replaced by something she could not read. She straightened, a single fist clenched in triumph.

Chapter Six
THE INEVITABLE

THE FIRST TWO WEEKS AT THE ACADEMY TAUGHT Aerin to fight past her fear, at least during classes. Despite the constant dread that she would give herself away, she forced herself to raise her hand and speak up. She *would* make the most of this opportunity and prove that she deserved to be here, for however long it lasted.

And prove it she did, consistently earning the top spot on the daily posted rankings for every academic class. Except debate.

Not that she didn't try to lead that course as well. She spent hours combing the library and searching the network, hoping to fill the gaping holes in her background knowledge about the Alliance and current events. She pored through history books, news bulletins, and instant postings. Nothing helped.

Because nothing prepared her to defeat Dane Madousin.

He had won every debate thus far. And today was unlikely to be an exception. Aerin watched him from the corner of her eye with irritation. As always, he appeared relaxed. The rattling of his pen against his chair was the only sign he was even awake.

The rest of the class, meanwhile, waited in stark silence, anxious over the looming announcement of the day's topic. Hands gripped the sides of desks. Teeth gnawed on fingernails. Gazes fixed on the teacher at the front of the room.

Xioxang also waited, his infamous stare pinned to Dane's pen. For a moment the rattling grew louder, then came to an abrupt stop. And the teacher's stare lifted, now taking in the entire class. Aerin hated that stare, the way those gold eyes dug into her skull. Prying.

Finally Xioxang announced the topic, carefully, as though presenting his students with a tube of nitroglycerine. "Has the Alliance achieved its objective in Wyan-Ot?" he asked, then glided into a corner.

Again with Wyan-Ot. The military action on that one small planet had already taken up four class periods. "Yes," Aerin said, not quite keeping the indifference from her voice. "The Allied military began withdrawing troops a few hours ago." She had checked the network that morning and read the most recent postings.

"Yeah," added a tall boy who was clearly anxious to prove he had read them as well. "We forced the infiltrators out of power." A grin stretched across his pasty face. "And we've started sending diplomats to help set up a new government."

Dane, of course, opened his mouth. *Two people with the same opinion,* Aerin thought sarcastically. *He couldn't allow that.*

"I fail to see how winning validates the decision to invade a planet," he said, letting his pen fall to his desk with a thud.

"Will you get off that, Madousin?" The pasty boy made a rude gesture under his desk. "It wasn't an invasion."

"And you're not the hind end of a—"

"Enough." Xioxang emerged from his corner long enough to send a glare in Dane's direction. Though the teacher's voice was stern, Aerin could not help but notice the faint glimmer of a smile at the edge of his lips. "The topic is not whether the Alliance was correct in sending soldiers to Wyan-Ot but whether the objective has been met."

"It hasn't," Dane replied.

"How can you say that?" argued Aerin. She felt too ignorant to either reject or condone the Allied action on the planet, but it seemed pointless to dismiss the success of the mission. "The entire conflict lasted less than eight weeks."

"I'm not saying the military lost." Dane leaned his head back, tilting his face toward the ceiling. "I'm saying it hasn't met the objective. And it's not going to meet it. Not in some minor battle on Wyan-Ot or any other little planet."

Protests suddenly filled the room. The other students thrust themselves into the conversation all at once. Their chairs scraped across the floor, and comments hurtled in Dane's direction. Aerin looked around, startled. How could a simple remark cause such a strong reaction?

Dane, himself, appeared neither surprised nor disturbed by the protests. If anything, he seemed to enjoy them. Instead of trying to field the barrage, he waited for it to subside, then picked up the earlier thread of the debate. "Look, why did the Allied soldiers go there in the first place?" he asked.

When no one else responded, Aerin replied, "Because the Trade Union tried to take over the Wyan-Ot government."

"Exactly. The real conflict is with the Trade Union, not the Wyannese. We all knew the Allied military could defeat the Wyan Army. But Wyan soldiers didn't cause this problem, and defeating them hasn't solved it."

He had a point.

Yvonne, her eyebrows arched, turned around in the front row. "So you think we should attack the Trade Union?"

"No."

"Madousin, you don't make any sense," said the pasty boy. "You can't say the Trade Union is to blame and then argue against attacking them."

Was he kidding? One thing Aerin had learned over the last two weeks was that Dane could argue against anything from any side. It was impossible to tell where he really stood.

"Look," Dane said. "The Trade Union is the source of the

problem. They've been sending representatives to convince other planets to join them for the last three decades."

"Spies," said Yvonne.

"Whatever you want to call them—"

"My parents say there's no doubt about what to call them," she cut in. "They use bribes and blackmail."

"Miss Entera," Xioxang interrupted, "when your parents join this debate, they can make their own points."

Yvonne stiffened.

"There's no doubt the representatives use questionable practices," Dane continued, "and that once a planet joins the Trade Union, the planet cuts off all ties to the Alliance."

"Yeah, yeah," said the pasty boy. "None of us are disputing that, Madousin. Get to your point."

"I have two points. One is that this is nothing new. The Trade Union has been doing this for three decades, and not once has the Alliance chosen to act until now."

He was right. Aerin remembered reading about the Trade Union's startling growth, especially in the last sixteen years, during which it had expanded from one to three star systems. Begun by a handful of wealthy planets incensed at the Alliance's moral restrictions on trade, the Trade Union, with its shady political practices and emphasis on privacy, had grown to become the largest single nation outside the Alliance. And frankly, she found it hard to blame the Council for being concerned.

"Why now?" Dane kept talking. "Why salvage a planet

like Wyan-Ot when we've ignored the same type of corruption on twenty or thirty other planets."

Because this planet is right outside the Allied boundary? Aerin hypothesized. Though the Trade Union's leaders had never openly threatened the Alliance, it was clear their biggest goal was to crush the nation they viewed as their main competition.

"Because Wyan-Ot is our primary source of ironite," said Yvonne. "And we don't want to lose access to another mineral-rich planet like Mindowan. Our resources are already thin."

Aerin frowned. Over the past two weeks, she had learned that the black metal used to build the Wall and the rotating tower known as the Spindle was called ironite, but until now she had never associated the substance with the conflict on Wyan-Ot.

"All right," the pasty boy said to Dane. "So what if we want to protect our access to ironite? It's vital for space age construction. Without it we lose economic and, therefore, political power against the Trade Union. Since when is it a crime to protect our resources?"

"It isn't," replied Dane. "But it doesn't solve the real problem. The Trade Union is still sending out its representatives and still refusing to work with us."

"So why not go after the Trade Union?"

Aerin felt a chill run through her body at the thought of an armed conflict between the two strongest nations in the universe.

"Because," Dane said drily, "we could all die."

* * *

Anger ricocheted off the walls. The room fairly boiled with passion, something Dane took no small amount of credit for. Gone were the raised hands of the first day of debate. Shouts sailed toward him, missed their target, and cascaded off the ceiling.

Enjoying the uproar, he shifted in his seat, trying to lessen the contact between the back of his chair and his most recent bruise. His gaze landed on the culprit. For sixteen days Aerin Renning had knocked him on his backside every afternoon in physical combat.

The bruises were nothing. He could handle the school's physical toll.

What had surprised him was the mental one.

He had *intended* to slide through his stint here. It was one thing to slack off when he could have been at the top of his class. But it was quite another to do so when someone else had the upper hand. Aerin had earned the top scores on the first science and lit tests of the year, due in part, he suspected, to a photographic memory and the fact that she seemed to live in the library. But that failed to explain her ability to analyze. Or her performance in technology, where she blew everyone away. Zaniels had even named her his assistant and given her the access code to the precious tech lab.

Not that Dane could not compete. He dominated debate, as well as most of the outdoor classes. But staying at that level was work. He had to study, and he had to train; and still she kept flattening him in physical combat, an ability that absolutely blew his mind. With awe. Though he couldn't seem to get close enough to her to express it.

She had deflected his attempts at personal conversation. In truth, from what he had observed, she avoided almost all social contact. There was something disjointed about her. She could connect thoughts that even teachers struggled to see, quote huge passages of text without notes, and dissect the themes in a book with painstaking detail. But every now and then she would fail to answer a simple question or go silent and watch her classmates with sharp intensity. Like right now. Why was she sitting there, quietly looking uncomfortable, when everyone else was upset?

For a split second, her dark eyes met his. And he struggled with what he saw there. Admiration? If she agreed with him, why not say so?

She was hiding something.

And he was running out of time to find out what.

"Mr. Madousin"—a scratchy voice from the intercom broke into his thoughts—"you have a call in the message room." The other students froze. The secretary never interrupted class, certainly not to announce personal calls.

Unless the caller is on the Council. Dane felt an ominous darkness sink through his chest and settle in his stomach. His deadline had come. He had known his father would return any day now. Standing, Dane gathered his supplies, certain he would not be back.

His classmates remained silent as he left. As if they had suddenly remembered who his father was, something they had managed to forget over the past few minutes.

Dane made his way across the hall. He wrestled open a stubborn door and climbed a narrow, sagging stairway into the darkness. The message room was under the eaves, a small, windowless space. At the far end of the room, a subtle ivory glow gave off the impression of a screen.

No use putting off the inevitable. Dane punched the Input button.

His father's image appeared, his rigid frame towering larger than life upon the wall. Pale skin matched the lips pressed tightly together. Sharp lines traced the smooth forehead, straight nose, and strong chin. The sound of breathing hissed over the speakers. Then the figure drew forward, just close enough for the row of gleaming medals on his uniform to sharpen into focus. "Well?" The word rang with tension. "Shall I tell them, or shall you?"

Dane slouched in silence against the left wall, knowing the lack of respect would grate hard after two months of *yes, sirs* and *yes, Generals.* He let his gaze peruse the empty corners of the ceiling.

"I suggest you answer," came the command. The faintest movement drew Dane's eyes back to the screen. A knuckle popped as his father's index finger pressed against his thumb.

Just waiting for you to tell me who it is I'm supposed to tell what.

The knuckle spiked. "You will inform Dr. Livinski immediately."

And what am I supposed to tell her? wondered Dane, keeping his face blank.

The chest with the medals expanded. "A man admits when he is guilty of a crime."

Oh, that was great. Dane forced laughter into his voice as he finally spoke aloud. "What am I being charged with now? Murder or manslaughter?"

"You and I both know you could never have fairly earned your way into that school." The words were like frozen nitrogen.

Dane turned away, back toward the stairs.

"You will admit you cheated on that entrance test, or I will do it for you."

Leave it to the General to question my intelligence by accusing me of cheating on the securest exam ever invented. "You would."

"I mean it, Daniel!" The words hammered at the back of Dane's neck. "And you can pack your bags. I want you out of that school and back on Chivalry before my ship lands in forty-eight hours."

Blindly Dane slammed the Off button. He had not expected to feel like this, as if somehow he had lost. How was that possible? He had known he would be pulled from the school as soon as his father returned from Wyan-Ot. The General still nursed a grudge against the academy, a grudge that dated back for unknown reasons even before Dane's brother Paul's rejection. And if that had not been enough, there was always the excuse of Dane's disobedience. But Dane had not expected this—to be forced to leave under some false accusation.

A slow whirr ebbed behind him, and the light in the room began to fade.

There was no doubt who the principal would believe. Even if Dr. Livinski were not his father's colleague on the Council, she would never listen to the word of a juvenile delinquent over that of a general.

Pitch darkness descended on Dane's shoulders. His palm pressed flat against the wall; his body refused to shift. *Return to Chivalry.* He didn't want to think about what that meant. Military school, most likely. Back under his father's control. There was no way out, not without an academy degree.

When he did finally move, his ankles screamed, and sharp spikes shot up from his wrist; but the pain did not matter, because he had made up his mind. He might never have had the power to stay at Academy 7. But he sure as hell had the power to decide how he left.

Chapter Seven
THE CRIME

THE GARDEN CALLED TO AERIN, THREADING ITS
seductive message through the cracks in her bedroom
window. *I can hide you,* the night seemed to say, and Aerin
slipped from her bed to lift the glass. A warm breeze rushed
inward, ruffling the sleeves of her rumpled uniform, and a
wonderful shudder of pointed leaves swished on all sides.
Thin clouds drifted across Academia's two moons. Without
conscious thought, she leaned out to breathe the rich scent
of maple. Her arms wrapped around an outstretched branch
and pulled the rest of her body out the window.

The maple's trunk had overgrown with branches, and Aerin
soon found places to prop her bare feet. Those feet, hard with
calluses, scarcely felt the prick of sharp twigs. *I suppose I should*

have put on my boots, came the belated thought as she glanced up several yards toward the open window.

But the rush of escape felt too good. Discarding the notion, she scaled down the rest of the trunk and swung with ease to the ground. Her feet moved with purpose, deeper into the tangle of the garden. Though she had not consciously planned to leave the dorm tonight, her mind had gone over this scenario a dozen times since her first sighting of the maple's outstretched branches. And she had known exactly where she would go since her first day of classes.

It took her fifteen minutes to find the circular fountain. Not because she had trouble placing it but because she wanted to enjoy the peace of walking amid the protective oak and pungent cedar. For this moment, at least, no one knew where she was. After her fright on the *Fugitive,* Aerin had thought she never wanted to be alone again, but she had learned that living among strangers could be more isolating than deep space.

The fountain's soothing song reached her eardrums and pulled her out from the rim of foliage. She moved across pavement, closer and closer until mist formed damp beads on her nose and cheeks. *I don't want to be alone. But how do I stop?*

The other first-year girls seemed to cluster around Yvonne, who had made it clear from the very beginning that Aerin did not belong. There was something frighteningly similar between the olive-skinned beauty and the guards back on Vizhan. She had a keen eye for others' weaknesses and a killer instinct.

Then there was Dane. Who was always watching. At first, Aerin had feared he would again target her, but today he had made himself the target in debate. She had not understood what he was doing, stoking the emotions of his classmates, until the other students had risen up in fury. And while she was not at all certain she agreed with his argument, the way he had faced down the entire class had been almost . . . gallant.

To wash away the thought, she reached a tentative hand toward the running water. Cool liquid streamed over her fingers and soaked the black sleeve of her uniform. Though the school had given her nightclothes, she could not bring herself to wear them. They made her feel unprepared.

She had never before had real nightclothes. Just an old shirt of her father's. For a moment Aerin let herself remember that shirt, the way the soft material used to hang below her knees and the way it smelled, of chocolate and caramel. Like her father.

No! She pushed away the thought and stepped back from the fountain. But the night no longer protected her, and memories of her father escaped the locked box in her mind where she had buried them. Images flooded her head, all of him: lifting her up so she could steer the trade ship; telling her long, exaggerated stories; thanking her for fixing the computer.

Her body shivered, now cold despite the warm air, and she squeezed her eyes tight. Nothing could keep the feelings from following the images: the softness of her father's touch when he bandaged a cut; the roughness of his whiskers when he forgot to shave; the way he made her feel—happy to be with him, mad when he ordered her around, worried when he slipped into a trance. But always, *always* safe.

And then the bone-crushing, mindless loss when he was gone. And she wasn't safe. And she didn't know if she would ever feel safe again.

Aerin sank down, burying her head in her hands, pressing her elbows to the cement. She mustn't; she mustn't; she mustn't—

But she had already begun. And there was nothing left to do but relive her father's death in the crash: his blood dripping from his forehead to the control panel of the ship; the twisted tilt of his neck; the empty, frozen gaze in his eyes. She crouched there for an eternity, fighting her demons and not crying. She had not cried in the six years since his death and did not remember how, but she remembered enough to keep her there, her body shaking and shivering, by turns, until a soft glow lit the sky and she could once again bury the memory.

Her sleeve had dried on her skin, and her eyelids weighed down. Aerin tried to get up. Her legs cramped, not wanting to unfold. She leaned back and stretched each limb, one at a time, then finally stood.

Careful to avoid sharp stones and brambles, she picked her way through the garden and back to the ancient maple. Towering above her, it lacked some of its allure. Working her fingers to make certain they could clench a fist, she began to ascend.

The climb took three times longer than the descent. Every twig seemed to catch her hair. Her footing slipped twice, and she knew her body was responding to the night's trauma. How dare her feet betray her!

With a final effort, she swung through the open window and landed in a crouch on the bedroom floor. *At last.*

Relief was short-lived.

"Ahem." A low sound yanked her upright.

The door was wide open. And in the gap stood Mr. Xioxang, a deep frown etching his thin face. For seconds he remained still, perhaps as stunned as she was. Then the frown cracked, and a harsh order whipped forth. "You will come with me to the Great Hall, Miss Renning. Immediately."

Briiing! The harsh sound shrieked in Dane's brain. Not his alarm clock; he had not set it.

Dane rolled over, burying his head under the pillow.

The shrieking did not subside. Not a clock at all. A dorm fire drill? He considered lying there until the drill was over, but then memories from his recent nightmares came back— smoke clogging his lungs.

He rolled out of bed, the floor clobbering his knees. More

bruises to go with the ones he already had. He reached up for the light, but the bulb would not turn on. Fighting the urge not to slump back to bed, he staggered to his feet. Then shouts in the hallway drew his attention.

"Lockdown!"

"You can't be serious!"

"They can't!"

"They can and they—"

Sheer force of will brought Dane hobbling to the Exit button. It failed to work. Overpowering the controls, he thrust open the door and stared out.

At a strangely still crowd. Other male students crammed this end of the hall. They had moved toward the stairwell, leaving behind a row of open doors, yet the exodus had ceased to flow. Bodies slumped against the walls, some of them dressed in uniform but most, like Dane's, in a haphazard mix of sleepwear and bare skin.

"What," he groaned, "is going on?"

"We're in lockdown," came an answer in a female voice.

Dane's head snapped in the voice's direction. At the entrance to the stairway, her slender body draped across the exit, was Yvonne Entera. What was she doing in this wing?

"Lockdown from what?" Thoughts flashed through Dane's mind, all drilled into him from a lifetime on a military base. *Attack? Invasion?*

But the girl flipped her hair over her shoulder. "It's for the

Council's protection," she said, "not ours. Someone broke into the tech lab last night."

Of course.

"We're all trapped in here," she said, "together, until Zaniels secures the files." She pushed away from the door and took a step in Dane's direction, but her path was blocked by a towheaded boy wrapped in a blanket.

"Why would the Council care about a bunch of school files?" asked the boy, showing no inclination to move.

Yvonne gave him a dirty look. "We all know there are more than *school* files at Academy 7. What do you think is the purpose of the Spindle?" She referred to the black rotating tower. "You don't really believe it's solely for decoration. What better place would the Council have for storing classified information?"

Rumors. Dane schooled his face not to react to her claims.

She flicked her fingernails. "My parents say we should all be on the lookout for spies, in case the Trade Union sends someone here to infiltrate the Alliance."

Her habit of quoting her parents annoyed him. As far as he was aware, the Enteras had inherited their position of standing, not earned it through some special insight. The planet of Entera had been named after the current family's ancestors, who had funded its initial exploration, not completed it themselves.

"The spy would have to be a hell of a flyer to navigate the entrance to the Spindle," said the boy in the blanket. "Even the best pilots in the universe would think twice about entering that moving black tube."

Murmurs of agreement filled the hall.

"Besides," said the boy, "I don't see what the Spindle has to do with the computer lab break-in."

"Obviously the *Council* thinks there's sensitive information in the school database as well," said Yvonne, finally negotiating her way past him. "I assume they know. So we're all in lockdown until Zaniels can prove nothing's been compromised."

"You mean until Livinski tracks down the culprit," said Dane.

"No." Yvonne closed the remaining gap between him and herself. "Dr. Livinski already knows who broke in. It doesn't take a high A.E.E. score to figure out that only one student had access."

What was that supposed to mean?

She gave him a smug smile. "Xioxang was here this morning to arrest her."

Her?

"Who?" demanded Dane, a cold suspicion slowly filling the pit of his stomach.

"Don't be naïve." The slender girl curved her blood-red fingernails around his arm possessively. "We all know which student has the best tech skills on campus. Zaniels even gave her an access code to the lab."

Chapter Eight
ACCUSATION

AERIN FAILED TO HEAR THE DOOR OF THE EMPTY basement room *click*, but she knew she was locked in. The cement floor, blank walls, and stark, stained ceiling all closed inward, pulled by the magnetism of her own fear. She felt her mind and body shut down, her muscles tighten, her limbs grow rigid. The dim light crumbled to darkness, blackness seeping beneath the inner layer of her skull and the outside of her cranium.

Whether Xioxang would return, she did not know. What she did know was terror, the bone-numbing terror of being cornered. Would they send her back to Vizhan and the slow torturous death of a runaway? Or would she face prison? Aerin knew little enough about Allied legal justice, but she knew prison was worse than death. Slave owners sent you there if they thought you were hiding something. And the screams that echoed from the cells were the screams of torture victims. No one ever came out alive.

She should have run, should have avoided capture at all cost, should not have followed Xioxang over here to the Great Hall in a useless stupor. How much did he know? Had he known everything before arriving in her dorm room? Or had her late-night adventure tipped him into doing a background check? No answers came. Only the blackness. And the knowledge that she was trapped.

Time became an enemy. She could not sense it. Or track it. Or force it to an impenetrable halt. It lurked relentlessly out of reach.

Until a tussle of sound crept along the ridge of her awareness, then shifted. "You should think about the circumstances in which I found her." The sharpness of Xioxang's voice sent a chill beneath Aerin's flesh. He must be standing guard outside the room.

"I have no say." The second voice vibrated under strain. "If the files have been tampered with, the solution is out of my hands." Aerin could not help but shudder as she recognized the second speaker: Mr. Zaniels, the one teacher she had almost trusted. So he, too, served as her jailer.

Again darkness swallowed her whole. Seconds or minutes or hours passed, her face and feet going numb before dialogue jolted back into her conscience.

"We should get on with this," said Xioxang.

"We can't. Livinski wants to handle it."

"That was before she started fielding angry calls from parents."

The words sliced through Aerin's brain. *Angry calls.* Everyone knew then: the parents, the teachers, the members of the Council.

"I have better things to do with my time than wait. It doesn't take an expert to question someone," Xioxang growled.

A glacial female voice cut through the complaint. "Perhaps your expertise would be better employed upstairs seeing that I am not disturbed." The command shattered the dialogue.

"Yes, Dr. Livinski."

"Oh, and Mr. Xioxang, no more calls . . . from anyone."

At the sound of fading footsteps, Aerin allowed a thin stream of air to exhale from her lungs. At least the hawk with his probing stare would not be present for her interrogation.

Then light slammed into the room. Her chest lurched as she clamped her eyelids shut and pressed her back against the wall. Clicking skidded over her eardrums. "The bulb must be out," came the smooth voice. "Come here, Miss Renning."

Aerin cracked her protective lids wide enough to make out the rigid figure in the doorway. The square-cut jacket, straight skirt, and tight bun left no room for leniency. Lips pressed together with a hint of disgust around the edges. For the first time, Aerin understood the power behind this woman. As a Council member, Dr. Livinski could condemn an entire nation with an accusation. It would cost her nothing to condemn one person.

"I assume you know why you are here," said the principal.

Aerin worked her jaw without sound. A single word might serve as her own betrayal. *Fool*, she chided herself. *They know already.* Still, she could not bring her tongue to attempt a defense for her illegal presence at the school.

"Come. Here." The principal spoke each word slowly, then raised an eyebrow. "Unless you prefer to remain in the dark."

Somehow Aerin pried her body away from the back wall. Numb legs staggered, and she stumbled forward. Long fingers gripped her by the elbow and, to Aerin's surprise, led her not only out of the room but straight into the tech lab.

The buzz of the computers, once a comfort, now hissed around her with sharp discord. She flinched at the sight of Zaniels looming beside his personal computer, arms crossed over his bulky chest. Anger marred the typically kind face.

But the dark expression moved past her as his gaze focused on the nearby machine. "Someone broke into the academy files last night," he said, "from this computer."

The grip on Aerin's elbow loosened. "You wouldn't have any idea how such a feat might be accomplished?" asked the principal.

Aerin felt her mouth drop open. Was this why she was here? Because they thought she had compromised school security? If this was all—

Then the hopeless insanity of the situation struck her. If

she admitted to knowing how to bypass security, there was nothing to keep them from thinking she had broken into the lab, and if she denied it, there was nothing to convince them she was telling the truth.

Unless she could prove someone else had hacked into the machine. "I might . . ." she tried to speak. "I might be able to track the culprit."

Zaniels glanced at the principal.

The look was unclear, but Dr. Livinski gave a slow nod, then made a sharp gesture toward an empty chair. "By all means," she said.

Aerin sat down, nerves firing along the short hairs up and down her arms. She might trace the hacker, but then again, she might not. If he or she had equal skill, there would be no trace to define the culprit and perhaps not even a path to unravel.

Her fingers moved slowly over the keyboard, paused half a second, then circumvented the password. The back of her mind screamed out that she had just given them proof of her own ability to break in.

But the risk was calculated. She had no hope without taking it, and this might be her only chance to clear her name, at least before they began a real investigation.

At her side, Zaniels grunted, but Dr. Livinski remained silent. Aerin did not dare look at either of them. She could not afford to gauge their reactions. Her full attention focused on the screen and the clues revealed there.

She did not have to look very hard. The hacker's path opened with startling ease. To her relief. And her growing anger.

Had the terror she had gone through this morning been due to nothing more than a silly prank? The hacker had entered a dozen restricted sites without any attempt to scroll for information or disguise the path. If she was not mistaken, he had even taken a few extra measures to ensure being caught.

And it was a *he,* of that she had no doubt, nor was there any question who had done the searching. Her temper boiled under her skin. How exactly like him! To waste all that energy and effort getting nowhere. It was maddening. And the most maddening thing of all was that he had somehow dragged her into it, because here she was, with the proof right at her fingers, capable of printing up his whole ridiculous route in a matter of seconds.

Except she suddenly did not care for the idea of telling. This had been no crime, really, and there was something infuriating about the way the culprit begged to be caught.

When she finally looked up, the principal was gone. Zaniels, perhaps too nervous to watch, had moved to a far corner where he paced back and forth. "Any luck?" He gave a grim smile.

Her throat felt dry, and her gut rebelled, but she could not dismiss the horror of the dark room.

Then Dr. Livinski stepped back into the lab. "Well, Miss Renning, do you know who broke into the database?" The icy voice and cool facade demanded a response.

Aerin opened her mouth . . .

Then closed it.

Less than two feet behind the principal stood the shadowy outline of a human form. And not just any human: with shoulders slouched, hands in pockets, head tilted to the side. She knew that look, the deceptively relaxed stance of Dane Madousin.

His dark eyes swam into view and for one endless moment met hers.

Aerin had a sudden vision of him fending off the entire debate class. She pushed it away. She owed him nothing. Nothing! This entire nightmarish morning was his fault. He deserved everything he had coming to him and more.

So why didn't she do it? Why didn't she tell Dr. Livinski the culprit was standing right behind her at this very moment? Why *was* he standing there?

The answer came in jagged memory, ripping its way down Aerin's chest. He wanted to remind Aerin that if he went down, she was going down, too, all because she had shown him that stupid shortcut their first day of class. Hadn't he threatened her that same day?

She hated him. With a passion.

"I asked you a question, Miss Renning." The principal stepped closer. "Do you know who broke in here last night?" The words hung in the air.

Aerin's eyes riveted on Dane's.

"No," she said.

Silence cluttered the space between them.

The response in his gaze was not what she had expected. He blinked, shook his head, then furrowed his brow as if trying to figure something out.

The principal's question rang with sarcasm. "You're certain?"

"Now wait a minute," said Zaniels. "She's done what we asked. If she says she doesn't know, she doesn't—"

"She knows," Dr. Livinski snapped. "Madousin confessed not three minutes ago, and according to that confession, Miss Renning showed him how to bypass the security code herself several weeks ago. I'm not sure what I find more reprehensible, a student who breaks into school property, or one who lies to cover up her own part in it."

Confessed? Aerin stared at Dane with shock. It made no sense.

"Listen, I didn't . . . that's not what I . . . it's not Aerin's fault." Dane struggled for words, something she had never seen him do in two weeks of debate. "She had nothing to do with this. You can't expel her just because—"

"Expel?" The principal gave a sudden turn. "Oh, believe me, Mr. Madousin, neither one of you is getting off that easy."

The light on Dr. Livinski's transmitter was blinking an hour later as she returned to her office. Red. The signal of the Council. *One interrogation finished. Now time for the second.*

She closed the door and pulled black shades over the glass walls. Visibility would not save her from this conversation. Reluctantly, she lowered the lights, then pushed the Input button.

The image of General Gregory Madousin shot onto a shade, his military jacket sporting every medal he owned, including the most recent, earned on Wyan-Ot. "Jane," he said, his face dark. "Our colleagues informed me of the lockdown."

"It's taken care of," she replied, the tips of her fingers settling on her desktop. "None of the files you are worried about were accessed."

"You can't know that."

Actually, she could. She had been perfectly aware of the fact ten minutes after sitting down at Zaniels's computer. But that had not answered how the young culprit had bypassed the security code, the discovery of which had been the entire purpose behind her investigation. She descended into her chair without breaking eye contact. "We have a trace of the entire path taken by the hacker."

"I want the culprit arrested." His chest puffed up like an Ondavan grouse.

"I can assure you there will be consequences." Dr. Livinski squelched the urge to tell him his own son was to blame. She had a firm policy about handling school discipline herself. Besides, she had spent more than enough time on the transmitter discussing Dane with his father the previous evening.

For the moment, however, the General's attention was consumed by someone else. His tone was a command. "I want every file related to the Traitor transferred."

Her hackles rose. She had known this would happen. The Traitor had been at the heart of Gregory's vendetta for more than fifteen years. "You already have the sensitive files," she said, squaring her shoulders. "I will not doctor school records."

"This is a political concern."

It's personal, she thought, *and you and I both know it.* "School records are my jurisdiction." Her fingers dug into the edge of her desk. She was not about to let him usurp her control of Academy 7.

"And my son is *mine.*" The image from the transmitter blurred.

"Not while he's attending my school." She was not going to have this conversation again, after four hours of it the night before. As the image cleared, he opened his mouth, but she cut him off. "I'll send you a scan of the trace, Gregory." And she severed the connection.

Her hand clenched on the closed transmitter. *Overprotective parents: always doing their best to undermine their children's education.* Already, she had wasted an hour that morning defusing the anger of Mrs. Entera, though how the woman had known about the lockdown had been a mystery until the admission that she had disregarded school rules by giving her daughter a personal transmitter. *Soon to be confiscated,* before the entire episode became a matter of public record.

Fortunately, upon reflection, Mrs. Entera had been none too eager to have the news of the lockdown, and with it her own deceit, released to the press.

And then—Dr. Livinski shoved the office transmitter across her desk—there was Gregory Madousin. She knew he had a grudge against her, and she could not entirely blame him for it, but that was no reason to forfeit his son's chance to attend the best school in the universe. Or to make the ridiculous claim that Dane had cheated on the A.E.E. Any parent that denied his or her child's accomplishments in order to win an argument was appalling.

Though Dane had certainly done his best to prove his father's point.

She sighed and pushed back her chair. She probably should have expelled the boy. But wouldn't Gregory have loved that!

And then there was the girl. Somehow as soon as Zaniels had mentioned his aide, Dr. Livinski had known Aerin would be tangled in this mess. The decision to question her had proven effective, though not in the manner the principal had anticipated. She had already identified Dane as the guilty party and had fully expected the girl to turn him in, after explaining how the boy had achieved his feat. But it had been Dane who had confessed.

Expulsion was not the answer. Dr. Livinski eyed the now clear, still light on the transmitter. A thin smile creased her lips. Those two students were going to have to work off every ounce of stress they had manufactured for her this day. And maybe, just maybe, if they spent enough time together, they could terminate Gregory's crusade against the Traitor. Though God help her when the general found out she was harboring Aerin Renning.

Chapter Nine
PUNISHMENT

CLEANING FUMES STUNG DANE'S EYES. DR. LIVINSKI'S view of punishment involved rags, metal pails, and ammonia water. A great deal of ammonia water. He wrapped his fingers around thin bucket handles and heaved the steaming pails up the narrow attic stairway.

"It's on your left." Xioxang's voice called from below, stabbing Dane's back. "Just before you reach the message room. No, your *left*."

Dane squinted into the darkness, trying to spot an Entry button. If he had not been told, he would never have known there was anything up here except the message room. The weight on his hands cut into his fingers, and it was just dawning on him that he was not going to be able to push a button even if he found one, when Aerin, laden with a tower of rags, swept around him and slapped the wall. And what must have been the button. A harsh squealing filled the air.

Then dust erupted. Dane coughed, the movement causing hot water to spill over a pail rim, scalding his thigh. He swore under his breath.

Aerin stepped forward, a dim stream of light illuminating her profile.

He blinked, startled by the vision. Her hair glimmered past her shoulders. Though still straight and mousy brown, the long tresses were no longer limp. And the skinny arms and legs he had observed on the first morning of class had somehow lost their sharpness. The exacting pace of Academy 7 must have agreed with her. That or the physical demands of knocking him on his ass every day.

"Move on, Madousin," came the harsh command from below.

Dane stumbled forward into a narrow room lined with dusty shelves. Grateful to relinquish both buckets onto the floorboards, he rubbed his aching fingers with his thumbs.

"Clean it up." Xioxang suddenly stood in the doorway. "Livinski wants every piece of memorabilia to shine.

Memorabilia? Dane squinted at the shelves. Sure enough, beneath the dust, cracked plaques fought for space with corroded trophies.

"What's the matter, Madousin?" the teacher challenged. "Never learned to perform physical labor?"

Dane did not dignify that with a response. Two hours of

labor every day for the foreseeable future were less a purgatory than a reprieve.

What he could not fathom was why hell had not come for him. His father would not have given up on pulling his son from the school. Nor would the General have changed his mind. The only explanation Dane could devise for why he was still here was that Dr. Livinski had blocked his father's request for removal—that she had refused to let Dane leave because she wanted to inflict her own version of punishment. As the Council member in charge of education, she had that power. Still, Dane had never known anyone to—

Aerin interrupted his thoughts as she slid past him for a second time without speaking. She wrapped a rag around a bucket handle and snatched up the heavy pail with its steaming contents. Within seconds she had scaled the top of a ladder and begun scrubbing down trophies.

Xioxang raised an eyebrow. "At least one of you knows how to work." He plucked a plaque off a nearby shelf and thrust it into Dane's hands. "Get busy, Madousin. I'll be back in two hours."

Stomach clenched, Dane remained motionless, staring at the dingy photo on the old award. Then, discarding the plaque, he squared his shoulders and peered up at the figure balanced on the ladder. He might not mind this punishment, but the mandate that Aerin had received it as well bit into his conscience.

She did not deserve to be here. The moment when the

principal had asked her who was to blame came back to him. Aerin must have known he was guilty. He had left a trail like a blazing meteor. But she had not turned him in, and, in the process, she had obliterated his whole concept of bravery.

"Listen—" His voice scraped over the word. What could he tell her? That he'd let his desire for revenge take precedence over everything else, including her reputation. Of course, he had never meant to involve her, but he might have realized the possibility if he had taken the time to think. After his father's accusation, nothing else had entered Dane's mind. He couldn't tell her that. Or explain. Could manage nothing more than the wholly inadequate, "I'm sorry."

The only response was the unforgiving sound of water dripping into a bucket.

For Aerin, the first five weeks of work crew were defined by silence. She intended to punish Dane. For dragging her into his stupid prank, for risking her future, and for failing even to attempt an explanation. His stilted apology in the trophy room that first day had displayed little more than a vague regret. He had no idea of the horror she had experienced in that empty basement room or what he had almost cost her. And she could not tell him. So she punished him, refusing to speak to him outside of class.

Back on Vizhan, silence had been her refuge, a place she could go where no one could defeat her, but something had changed. Her involvement in the *crime,* as the other students now referred to the tech lab incident, had placed her squarely at the center of the school's gossip mill. The other students all watched her now with wary stares. Yvonne and her close-knit clique stepped off paths and curved around Aerin in giant semicircles. At meals, they convinced others to avoid her table. The barrier Aerin had built to protect herself had expanded beyond her control, and the whispers and smothered laughter hurt.

It took her a week to admit that she cared.

It took another four before she realized that punishing Dane was making matters worse. The two hours she spent every day beside him—scrubbing, dusting, painting, pruning, and doing three times the amount of work he accomplished—had become sheer torture. Her refusal to speak seemed not to disturb him at all. Or to dissuade him from talking. On and on, he yammered, complaining about everything: the floor was too hard, the paint too thin, the pruning scissors too rusted. He *never* stopped.

Still, she clung to the security of silence. Until the day Xioxang ordered Dane and Aerin to wash the outer windows of the Great Hall. Buckets in hand, they headed with caution around the front of the building toward the south side. Usually this section of the lawn cleared out after classes, but with fall exams looming, the shooting hours for upper classmen had been lengthened. Targets scattered the field, and a number of older students gathered nearby, choosing lasers.

The slight breeze turned to frost in Aerin's chest as she

spotted the gleaming compact firearms. Every nerve in her body reacted to those weapons, and the barrels that had tracked her every move in the fields on Vizhan.

In front of her, a boy raised his laser as if it were part of his hand, aimed at a target, and fired. *Pow!*

The sound pierced Aerin's flesh. She jumped.

Someone touched her elbow, and she jerked away, swinging an instinctive backhand.

Dane dodged, dropping his bucket and sending her a strange look. Then he shrugged as if giving up on understanding her and proceeded forward.

Aerin followed him, pinning her gaze between his shoulder blades. She tried to block out the sound of the shots as she made her way along the edge of the practice field.

Her focus worked, perhaps too well, for when Dane stopped and she allowed herself to look elsewhere, the massive structure overhead took her by surprise. She felt her jaw drop as she gazed up at the scaffolding of thin boards and rusted pipes stretching along the building's stone side like an unwanted fungus.

Her shocked stare must have given away her apprehension.

Dane took another step, clutched one of the corner poles, and gave it a shake. A shower of paint and dirt chips drifted down.

Lines furrowed his brow. "Ludicrous," he muttered, then ignoring both his own assessment and the built-in ladder, he wrapped his hands around the pole and began to scale it. He literally pulled his body thirty feet in the air, then dropped cat-like onto the highest platform. "I suppose if we die," he called down, "we won't have to finish washing the windows."

Aerin felt a certain amount of envy. Dane's coolness in the face of danger put her own attempts at subterfuge to shame. Her glint of admiration quickly faded, though, when she noticed he did not have his bucket.

She turned and peered back around the corner. The old metal pail waited, abandoned, on the far side of the practice field.

Pow! Pow! Pow! A new hail of laser shots fired.

Aerin gripped the pole at her side. *Forget the extra water. Mine is enough.* She was shaking.

"Afraid of heights?" The question came from above. Dane lay on his stomach, his chest and shoulders hanging over the platform's edge.

Idiot. She gathered her self-control, hefted her own bucket, and began climbing the ladder as quickly as possible. Reaching the top, she heaved her pail onto the platform with a resounding thud.

"Watch it!" Dane warned, then added, "You might want to stay on the sides. The center seems weak."

She took the creaking of the wood as confirmation and set to work without a word. All five windows at this level were covered with thick dirt. It washed off, but not without arm and shoulder muscle.

Dipping a rag into the same bucket, Dane also began to scrub, launching into a string of complaints against the Allied government for allowing the school to fall into such neglect. "Education, the backbone of the Alliance, my ass," he grumbled, mocking the line Aerin had first heard the captain of the *Envoy* say and since learned was a popular political quote. "If the government really valued education, do you think we'd be risking our lives to wash a few windows?"

Dane was nothing if not dramatic, she thought.

"Honestly," he continued, "if they'd redirect half the funds wasted on Wyan-Ot, none of the academies would have to choose between good teachers and a cleaning staff." He plunged his rag into the bucket and splashed the precious water over the platform.

Speaking of waste. Aerin glared at Dane. How could he complain about funding while he stood before her dressed from head to toe in his free school uniform?

She tried to tune him out, but the laser fire from below kept shredding her concentration, dragging her where she did not want to go, into memories she did not want to have, had never wanted to have, and had never truly managed to banish: the child she had seen shot for dropping a sack of grain, the woman who had outworked men half her age and been killed on her seventieth birthday, the guard who had pressed the barrel of his own laser to Aerin's head and ordered her to say when.

She was cold. The breeze up here was stronger than on

the ground, and the whistling along the pipes evoked that of distant screams. Her bare hands were chilled, and though she dipped them back in the warm water, they were shaking.

And then a volley of laser fire sent her entire body into a spasm.

"Damn it!" Dane shouted, his voice jerking her into the present. Water covered the platform and streamed off through the cracks.

Dimly, Aerin noted the fallen pail. She must have knocked it over. Embarrassment surged through her body, then exploded in a defensive attack. "Well, go retrieve *your* bucket!" she snapped.

He stared at her, eyes glittering. "It speaks," he said.

Only then did she realize she had just broken her silence. "It," she replied, "is sick of doing your share of the work." The sudden possibility of an argument channeled her energy and allowed her to focus on something other than the target practice below.

"Well, you certainly do more than your share of making a mess."

She sputtered, then let loose with a stream of swear words. "I wouldn't even be here without the mess you've put me in. You are a lazy, selfish, stubborn snob!"

"*I'm* stubborn? You're the one who's been scrubbing in silence for weeks. One wonders if you're even human."

"You!" She added a descriptive term and hurled her rag at him.

He sidestepped it.

Both of them watched the blue cloth sail thirty feet through the air to land in the grass. They breathed without words for a minute. Then a sound rumbled from his throat. For a second she thought he might roar at her, but instead the tone changed. It bubbled up, then erupted in unexpected laughter.

It made no sense. He had no right to be laughing at her.

Well . . . she had chosen rather an odd time to explode at him, seeing as she was the one who had knocked over the bucket. And it was rather childish to throw the rag. And . . . actually . . .

He had every right to laugh at her.

She slouched against a window, not certain how to respond.

He slumped down in a corner, lifted his own rag, and gave it a halfhearted toss in her direction. It missed. This produced a new wave of laughter, and he required another minute to control himself. Then, wiping a tear from his eye, he said, "I think I've been called a lot of things, but not a selfish snob."

She noticed he left out the term *stubborn*.

"Well, you are," came her response. "You're always arguing against the Alliance and the Council, your own father. You have no right."

"Excuse me?" The laughter slid from his face.

"You have everything: looks, money, freedom, a chance at a good education."

"How do you—"

She pushed off the wall, not about to listen to his excuses. "Do you have any idea how many people in this universe don't share those luxuries? No one threatens you. No one questions your right to exist. You have a future and the chance to learn at the best school in the universe." The passion was ringing in her voice now. "And you don't care! You don't care about anything!"

"That's not—"

"You risked it all, your future and mine, for nothing but a stupid prank!"

She stopped, her chest heaving.

Only then did she take in the effect of her words. Emotion swept Dane's face: surprise, defensiveness, anger. And something else, something that did not belong.

"What do you know about me, Aerin?" he said, his voice low. Then he stepped close. "You're not even from the Alliance . . . are you?"

The words were like a meteor shard plunging into her heart. Her life here, her place at the school, everything relied upon the myth that she was a citizen. And despite herself, she had begun to think she might succeed. The energy drained from her chest, her limbs. A sharp tingling began in her fingers, and she couldn't stay there, couldn't face the accusation that had just annihilated her dreams.

So she did what she always did, without thought or contemplation. She headed for the ladder, then over the edge, and down, her blood pounding in her ears. She needed escape. Nothing else mattered in the blur of the world. Nothing else existed.

Until the laser fire.

Pow! The sound ripped through her chest.

Her foot slipped. She lost her balance, and her fingers began peeling off the rungs.

But a tight, fierce grip suddenly clenched her left hand. She looked up at the fingers wrapped around her own, the white knuckles, cracked skin, and blue veins.

He didn't say anything, just waited for her to regain her footing. Then let her go.

Chapter Ten
AT RISK

SHE FLED, OF COURSE. ALL HER RESOLUTIONS TO STOP running had come apart, unraveling into a tangle as fine as shredded wire. Her thoughts were at war with themselves. How had he found out she was from outside the boundary, despite her secrets and silence, and after all this time? He could not have known before because he would have used it to threaten her.

Or would he? If he had been threatening her just now on the scaffolding, why had he caught her when she slipped? No one on Vizhan would have done that. The guards would have laughed at her own fallibility, and none of the other slaves would have risked it. To show empathy or love was to give the guards power over you.

This is the Alliance. Any decent human being—

But she had not thought of Dane as decent, not since that first day in the cafeteria when he had become her nemesis. She had not thought about that day in ages. She had just moved on, her focus on the future and facing down Dane.

Because of something Yvonne had said.

About his making fun of Aerin during debate. In fact, the gist of Yvonne's argument had been that he could not have meant what he said because he would never really criticize the Alliance with his father on the Council.

What nonsense! Dane had been by far the most outspoken critic of the Alliance all term. Less than half an hour ago, Aerin, herself, had accused him of failing to value the freedom he had here.

She slowed her steps, then pressed her head against the rough bark of a tree at the garden's edge. That first day of classes she had been a pawn, afraid of everything, and based on one conversation, she had made a snap judgment about a young man she really knew nothing about. Hadn't that also been part of today's discussion? Dane telling her she knew nothing about him. Yes, just before he threatened her.

And tried to save her life.

Even now she could feel the intensity of Dane's grip. If she had fallen, that grip would have stopped her. It had been that tight, that fierce. It had not been warm, or polite, or half-hearted in any way. It had squeezed her knuckles together in almost bone-cracking pain, and it would have held her up.

Maybe he had not meant to threaten her.

Or maybe he had. Maybe she should pack her bags right now and try to catch the first flight off the planet.

But she had nowhere to go. And no longer any desire to run.

Dane knew he had blown it. He could picture Aerin when she had left the scaffolding half an hour before, her face as drained of color as a snowbird in the moonlight. She had started talking! Five weeks he had worked at her side without so much as a "Please pass the water bucket," and now she had run off, her contradictory nature rushing to the forefront. One moment she was all fire, the next flight.

He could not regret his urge to laugh at her accusation. So she thought he was a good-looking spoiled snob. That was almost as rich as the fact that she was unafraid to say it to his face. But he had not meant to frighten her. He had only blurted out his realization of her foreign origin without thinking. *Stupid.*

Of course she would not want anyone to know. If she was here illegally, her place at the school would be in danger. Not that he would ever tell. But she didn't know that.

Devoid of water, Dane left off washing the windows and fetched plywood to repair the platform instead. He was on his knees, pounding the wood onto the scaffolding, and kicking himself mentally, when a shadow stretched over him. Dropping the hammer, he winced at the thud. "Aerin," he said.

"You didn't mean to blame me for the tech lab incident, did you?" Her response startled him.

He twisted around.

She looked worn, shadows rimming her dusky brown eyes. Her lips were cracked, and she was shivering. He had a strange desire to comfort her, but he knew better than to make any sudden movements.

"No, I—" Dane started to answer.

"And you didn't come to the lab that morning to threaten me?"

"Of course not."

She ran a hand against the peeled molding of a windowsill. "And you didn't intend to threaten me . . . that first day we were sparring in physical combat?"

Where was this going? He shook his head, now completely off balance, and lifted a knee off the plywood. "Why would I do that?"

"I'm not sure." Her voice vibrated just a bit. "I'm not sure why you would do those things. Or why you would make fun of me in class—"

What?

"—when you barely knew me. Or why you would break into a computer lab without taking the least trouble to cover your tracks."

He opened his mouth, then closed it.

"You wanted to be caught, didn't you?" Her words fell like glass splinters onto clean boards.

To argue would negate the truth of his other denials. His right hand flexed, reaching blindly for the hammer. Not there. Dimly he remembered that he had dropped the tool on his other side.

"Why?" She asked the question he had prided himself on avoiding.

"Why what?"

"Why try to get caught?"

He stood up, hoping the movement would give him confidence. It failed utterly. Sliding his hands into his pockets, he shrugged, providing no answer.

She was undeterred. "You must have assumed I would be blamed. You're not stupid."

Right. "Look, Aerin, sometimes when I'm angry, I don't think." How many times had Pete warned Dane against that exact failing?

"Why were you angry?"

He was not going to answer that, not for anyone. He had assumed his father would pull him from the school. The entire point of the break-in had been to preempt that fact and attract enough attention to embarrass the General. But the press had never gotten hold of the story, and, for some unfathomable reason, Dane was still here.

He and Aerin stood for a while, each looking at the other without really seeing. For Dane, the face in front of him, the pipes, the boards, even the massive stone building and the sweeping school grounds disappeared. His thoughts wandered around inside himself, careening down hidden passages and bumping into corners.

And judging by Aerin's eventual response, her thoughts traveled inward as well. She slumped down against a clean window and whispered, "I don't know why I do this to myself."

He waited, not sure what to say. Little of this conversation had made any sense, not that he had helped clarify things when given the chance.

The lull lasted another ten seconds before she lashed out at him. "I convinced myself you were the devil, you know!"

"No," he teased, "I'd never have guessed."

"And all the time . . ." She brought her hand to her forehead, then smoothed it back through her windblown hair. "You weren't thinking anything about me."

A grin clung to the corners of his mouth. That was more of an understatement than he cared to admit. "Actually, my backside has thought about you quite a bit."

She blinked.

"After physical combat," he explained, remembering the first time she had knocked the wind out of him. It had left him stunned. He had never met anyone who moved the way she did. But then she wasn't from here.

He took a deep breath, then dropped his voice. "I'm sorry I frightened you earlier. You really shouldn't worry, Aerin. You're one of the strongest first-years in the school. Everyone knows you deserve your place."

Doubt lay naked in her face. "Not everyone."

He squinted at her, trying to figure out who she meant. The principal maybe, because of the trouble he had brought down on her.

Then Aerin stammered, "How . . . how did you know I wasn't from the Alliance?"

He picked up a nail, turning it in his fingers and trying hard to keep a straight face, even though the memory brought back the same desire to laugh as before. "You were swearing at me in off-boundary slang."

Her hands clenched into fists.

"That was just a part of it, though," he added, feeling a sudden urge to explain. "I knew you must have learned those particular phrases outside the Alliance, but then I realized how much that might explain about you—about how you know so much about some things and nothing about others, like how to turn on a computer."

Her face burned a brilliant red. "How did you know it was off-boundary slang?"

He opened his hand, dropping the nail and staring at the red creases on his palm. "My father's on the Council, remember? He speaks a lot of languages."

She closed her eyes. "Stupid." Her voice was a whisper.

"Oh no, you don't," said Dane, pretending to take offense even though he knew she was deriding herself. "You told me a few minutes ago I wasn't stupid. You can't take it back now."

"Can't take it back." The words sank like water dripping down the pipes.

"Aerin, I have no intention of telling anyone you're not an Allied citizen." He held her dark eyes in his gaze, hoping to convince her he meant what he said, that he was telling the truth and there were no strings attached.

Well, perhaps one string. He held out the hammer. "Of course, if you felt like coming back to work, I wouldn't mind. This job might not ever end without you."

The hammer waited.

She looked right past it, then stood up, dusting off her perfectly clean uniform and letting her gaze sweep the perimeter. The humming of the wind filled the pause, and her hair blew out in long strands behind her neck. Then her hands rose to her hips. "Well, we wouldn't want to anger Dr. Livinski any more, would we?"

He cocked his head, noting the angle of her chin, the set of her shoulders, the distinct curve of her profile. At that moment, in that pose, she looked almost . . . regal. In a wild, untamed sort of way. "I don't know," he said. "I'm starting to think this punishment isn't all that bad."

The brown eyes shot down to his. "It's bad enough, thank you." And she plucked the hammer from his hand.

Chapter Eleven
BARGAIN

DANE SPENT THE NEXT COUPLE OF WEEKS FORMU-
lating a plan of action. He and Aerin now had a working
relationship. She asked him to hand her the occasional rag or
paintbrush. He refrained from griping. They even discussed
the quality of an assigned job now and then. None of this,
however, had improved his status in physical combat.

Fortunately there was no first-quarter exam in that particular subject. Dane made it through the tests he did have
with scarcely a speck of stardust on him. And judging by
the posted scores, Aerin made it through even more cleanly.
Not that anyone would know that by the way she continued
to bury her head in a book every spare minute of the day,
not lighthearted novels or required reading either, but thick,

heavy texts on historical, political, and social aspects of the Alliance. Dry and dull. The books, though, finally gave Dane the idea he needed for leverage.

He tracked her down in the library.

Personally, Dane had avoided the open room on the south end of the second floor as much as possible. He disliked the way the third-year students who manned the checkout counter could monitor everyone, whether the occupants were browsing the long shelves, downloading data from the information center, or studying at the rectangular tables in the study area.

Aerin, of course, was as far from the counter as possible. Despite the fact that a large table with comfortable chairs remained empty at a window to her left, she had ensconced herself in a small cubicle, her feet and knees propped up against the wooden desk, her chair tilted toward the wall. He wondered if she had chosen the position to thwart any person from sitting next to her.

Not that it would stop *him*.

Snagging a chair from a nearby table, Dane spun it around beside her and swung one leg over the seat. He leaned forward, resting his chin lightly on the chair back.

She ignored him, keeping her nose immersed in a thick tome, *The Evolution of the Alliance*. Perfect.

He snatched the book from her hands. "I have a proposition for you."

Her palms came down to the edge of the desk with a snap. "There are better ways of asking."

Maybe, but he had her attention now, didn't he? He pulled the book close, safely trapping its maroon cover between his chest and the chair's woven back. "I'm not asking. I'm making an offer."

She glared at him. "Now?"

Well, yes. "Doing a little light reading?" he asked, lifting the heavy book and drumming his fingers on the cover. She reached for the text, and he buried it once again behind the chair. "You don't need to work this hard, you know."

"What would you know about work?" she snarled.

"Oooh!" He held up a hand in mock surrender. "You think defeating you every day in debate is easy?"

The barb hit its target. Her chest deflated.

"I could help you." He inched the book just high enough for the title to peek over the edge at her. "Then you wouldn't have to read every incredibly dull, poorly written treatise in this library."

"Maybe *you* don't." She eyed him as if he had tainted DNA.

"What's that supposed to mean?"

"It means," she said, "you're Xioxang's favorite."

"Right." Casually he slid the chair closer and laid on the sarcasm. "Xioxang obviously has favorites."

"He always prefers your arguments in class."

"Because they're the best."

She did not deny it. In fact, judging by the way her thumb inched up to trace the rim of his chair, she was ready to listen.

"I could help you prepare an argument," he said.

"Maybe." Her voice dropped low. "But which one? The topics are random, and they can go anywhere. Don't you understand, Dane? When it comes to current events, I have no background, none at all. The stuff the rest of the class knows about the Alliance—I didn't grow up with that. It's one thing to do the reading for a class. It's another to defend myself against the unknown. No matter how much I read and study, there are some things I'll never learn that way."

"Exactly my point." He rocked back, inching the book higher still. "Why waste your time on the wrong stuff? I guarantee you half the students in that class don't know Karsky's ten evolutionary stages of the Alliance."

Her gaze shot to the author's name printed under the title of the book.

Yeah, I read it. How else would I know it was dull? "Look, Aerin, preparation is only half the challenge of winning a debate."

"And the other half?"

He had her now. "You have to choose the right side."

"Your side, you mean." She bristled.

"No, the losing side."

"What?"

"Always choose the weaker side."

"Why would I do that?" Doubt edged her voice, but now she was sitting erect, her feet flat on the floor.

"Because then you have further to go to prove your case." He eased the feet of his chair down. "In a debate, there are two sides. If both make a good argument, then the less popular side wins because that side had further to go to prove its point. Simple logistics."

"If you don't care which side wins." She frowned.

"It's a debate. It doesn't matter which side wins."

"You mean it doesn't matter to you." The tone in her voice unsettled him. Or maybe it was the fact that that her criticism disturbed him at all.

"It's a class," he said. "The point is to flesh out the different sides of an argument."

"And you don't care if the truth gets lost in the shuffle. Don't you believe in anything?!"

The students at a nearby table turned toward them, and one of the third-years at the checkout desk sent a glare in Aerin and Dane's direction.

"Of course I do," said Dane. *Why was she harping on this?*

She crossed her arms, lowering her voice. "What?"

His brow furrowed. This was not part of the plan. "What . . . do I believe about what?" He fumbled for his tongue.

"About anything." She rolled her eyes. "Start with the Alliance, since that's what you're offering to help me study."

For a minute, he scrambled with his thoughts, trying

to decide where to begin. Then his words came out slowly. "I . . . agree with the Manifest." And now he had begun, the explanation spilled out. "That we need a unifying force among the planets."

"And you believe the Alliance should be that force?"

"No— That is, the Alliance could be a model, but I don't believe a single government would be feasible for the entire universe."

"Then what do you mean by a unifying force?" She was really asking, not testing him. He could tell by the way the lines shifted on her face, questioning.

"I'm not sure," he answered. "Some type of venue for communication—a place we can talk about issues: trade, education, civil rights."

"Then you don't trust the Council to deal with those issues?" There was no judgment in the question.

Choosing his words carefully, he answered with as much honesty as he could. "I think the Council has done its best to deal with tough issues, Aerin, but they don't have the resources to fight every problem in the universe." *Or the perspective.*

"They seem to think they can take on the entire Trade Union."

He shook his head. "I don't believe the Council wants war with the Trade Union."

"Why? Because your father is traveling to the border next month for talks with their leaders?"

Dane shrugged. Let her interpret that as she liked.

She sat without speaking, then said something so softly he almost failed to hear it. "What do you want, Dane?"

He was starting to wonder that himself. No one had ever pried such an unguarded answer from him about his genuine views on the Alliance's future. Was bargaining with her really worth it?

She must have caught the confusion on his face. "In exchange for your help in debate," she clarified. "What do you want from me?"

Doubt faded, his grip on the heavy tome loosening. "I'm tired of getting trampled every day." He grinned. "Teach me to fight."

She snatched the book and headed toward the checkout counter. Her agile legs moved at a rapid clip. For a second, he thought he had lost. Then her head turned, long brown hair flying out to the left, and she hurled one last comment over her shoulder. "I accept. But you may regret it."

Regret was not the word Dane would have chosen to describe the next evening's tutoring session. Humbling. That was the word. His back hurt—and his shoulders, his neck, his collarbone, his spine, his ankles, his heels, his elbows, for goodness' sake.

With a sharp kick, Aerin sent him to the ground for the fourth time. The grassy practice field had long since failed to look soft. What was he doing wrong? He was balanced, prepared, patient: everything his instructors on base had taught him. But every time he stood up, she just wiped him out again.

"Stand," she ordered.

He struggled into opening position.

Aerin sliced out with her left leg. He spotted it, moved, and crashed into the backside of her right elbow. *Thwap!* The blow to his head sent him reeling.

"I told you, Dane, the key to a real fight is offense. If you react to my movement, I've got you on the ground. You want to finish a conflict within two, maybe three moves. It's not a sport. It's survival."

He eased his palm away from his throbbing ear. The planet's sinking sun, the side of the Great Hall, and Aerin all danced before him in a jumbled blur. He waited for them to stop before daring to speak. "Maybe we could limit this first lesson to below the neck. I'd like to survive."

The look Aerin gave him sent a clear response.

"Listen, you are the one who said you wanted this," she replied. "If you would rather not . . ."

"I want to learn," Dane confirmed.

She arched an eyebrow, moved toward him, and cracked a smile as he flinched away. "I won't hurt you."

His throbbing ear said otherwise.

Her hands dropped to her hips. "You have to train your

body to listen to your brain. It's not like preparing for a wrestling match or a sword fight. With those you can practice patterns so that your body will take over for you."

"My instructors used to say I needed to let my instincts guide me."

"I'm not saying you should ignore your instincts; they're giving you feedback. But the reason patterns work in sport training is because there are limits. Rules."

"Like not connecting above the neck?" Dane rubbed his ear.

"Like not connecting with the neck." She shifted closer to the nearby wall, rubbed a hand over its rough surface, and removed a small piece of crumbling stone. It had been her idea to practice in the Great Hall's evening shadow. She had thought they would draw less attention here. "The first thing a real attacker is going to do is aim for a part of the body that will inflict the most damage."

A chill crept through him. "I don't want to learn to kill someone," he said.

Her next words heightened the chill. "We don't often choose whether someone will try to kill us." Aerin hurled the stone against the wall and watched the gray rock shatter.

"I doubt Miss Maya would agree with your point of view."

"Then you underestimate her. Academy 7 is the school of choice for recruiting military officers, isn't it? She wants her students to stay alive."

He supposed Aerin was right. He had not been thinking of this as a military school. It was nothing like the Air Force Academy back on Chivalry, or the combat school his brother attended on Maravel 9. Here, students were taught to think for themselves, not follow orders. But just because Academy 7 had a broad focus did not mean the purpose behind its physical training was any less serious.

"Is that why you chose to come here?" Dane asked. "Because you wanted to learn survival skills?"

Aerin stared at the remnants of the shattered stone. "I came to learn how to do more than survive." She gave him a quick glance, then shifted into fighting stance.

"Enough for now," he said, backing away.

"You wanted this." The implied challenge ran thick in her voice.

He dropped to the ground and rolled back onto the deep soft grass. It was cool against his sweating skin. She stood uneasily, shifting her weight from foot to foot as if unsure what to do without a defined task. She was like a feral cat, he thought, ready to attack or flee at a hint of danger, but unable to relax. "Sit down." He pounded the flat of his hand on the ground beside him.

She sat.

He leaned his head back and let his chest rise and fall with the intake of oxygen. Academia's sun slipped over the horizon's edge, and the sea green sky shifted to a deep turquoise.

She did not say anything. No surprise there. She was wrapped so tight an untoward word might send her sprinting in the opposite direction, but he had an intense desire to learn more about her. After all, he was *still* here. She was the one who had been harping on him about throwing away his chances, so he might as well take her advice and begin by unraveling the mystery that was Aerin Renning.

"Where'd you learn to fight like that?" he asked.

Silence.

He gave up on her answering that question and tried another. "Where'd you grow up?"

Her head snapped in his direction. Too late, he remembered she had a reason to keep her origin a secret.

Well, he already knew she was not an Allied citizen. "Come on, Aerin, you practically had me give a speech yesterday on what I believe. The least you can do is tell me something about yourself."

She rocked forward to her knees. For an instant he thought she was leaving, but instead her fingers dug into the ground, tearing a patch of grass up by the roots. "I . . ." Her head dropped low, shoulder muscles twitching, and she inhaled a ragged breath. When she finally spoke, her voice wavered slightly above a whisper. "My father was an independent trader." *Past tense.* "He flew cargo between planets and space stations in the Dyan sector."

"But never in the Alliance?"

Another breath, this one less ragged.

"No. He never traded here. He never even mentioned the Alliance." Her head came up. "It's strange."

"He must have been gone from your home a lot if he flew a ship."

"I lived with him on that ship," Aerin replied, releasing the plucked grass. "You asked where I was from."

"You didn't have a home planet?" The idea was startling. Dane rolled to his stomach and peered up at her.

"Not that I can remember. We flew around a number of systems, but we never stopped on planet for more than a month."

"You didn't have any other family?"

"No."

And your father is dead now. The unspoken thought lay between them, the emotion in her voice making it obvious.

It was Aerin who broached the subject. "I . . . I haven't talked about him with anyone since he died."

Dane was unsure how to respond to that. He wanted to know about her, but if he listened to her problems, sooner or later she was going to want to know his. And there were things he had no desire to share.

"It isn't as hard as I thought it would be, talking about him," she said, belying the statement by plucking another handful of green.

Dane quelled a sudden desire to still her nervous fingers by taking her hand. "What was he like?" he dared instead.

"He could be funny," she said, "and spontaneous. He would

change course when it struck him. His customers didn't care for that, but he always smoothed things over with them. He could be very persuasive at times." She smiled, then her face fell. "Other times he would sit silent for long stretches, not responding to anyone."

"What about school?" Dane asked, hoping to distract her from whatever new sorrow had clouded her thoughts.

"My father taught me: physics, advanced math—he loved to read. He said reading was the soul's salvation."

"And how to fight?"

She shrugged.

Dane wondered how a lone trader on the fringe of society had gained enough educational background to prepare her for the A.E.E. "Your father must have gone to school himself then."

"Maybe."

Maybe? For growing up with only one person in her life, she lacked a fairly important piece of information. Why would this man have raised his daughter by himself on a trade ship in what was more often than not dangerous territory? The questions swirled.

Dane did not ask them, though, because Aerin chose that moment to turn the tables. "What about *your* father?"

And that was the end of the conversation.

Chapter Twelve
TOUCHSTONES

AERIN WAS REMINDED FREQUENTLY OVER THE NEXT two months that Dane was still exasperating: the way he drilled her on the small points of an argument, then turned and argued the flip side against her in class; the way he refused to use certain openings in combat, claiming that to do so went against his sense of moral conduct; the way he managed to let others' snide remarks slide past him as if they meant nothing.

If Aerin had been asked at the end of their second term to describe Dane, the first word she would have used would have been *maddening.* She would also have added *stubborn, intelligent,* and, to her surprise, *funny.* His sense of humor, couched in irony, took her a while to appreciate, but it was also bluntly honest; and, by the start of Academia's damp season, she found herself looking forward to his unvarnished opinions on every topic from flight paths to Ausyan philosophy.

There were no pedestals in Dane's world. No crystal vases to be treated with supreme care. No heroes. But there was a constant willingness to take out a topic, test it, shake it apart, mix up the pieces, and test them again.

Perhaps that's why he spends time with me, Aerin found herself thinking one afternoon as she negotiated the Great Hall's uneven stairs on her way to report for work. *Because I haven't made up my mind about this part of the universe.*

Dane's interest in her was baffling. Between work crew and tutoring sessions, he spent four to five hours with her every day after class. And she was not the only one who found his attention toward her unfathomable. More than once she had noticed Yvonne's black eyes surveying Dane while he was helping Aerin prepare an argument in the library. Or sitting with her during meals. She kept expecting him to lose interest and turn his attention toward the Entera beauty, but—

"Where is he?" Xioxang suddenly swept out of his classroom, cutting off her train of thought. Red robes billowed behind him, and the folds of his hood shadowed his face.

Aerin defended Dane. "He's helping Miss Maya put away supplies at the south end. He'll be here in a few minutes."

"Then you can tell him not to report for work today." Xioxang lifted his head with a sharp movement.

"Miss Maya asked him for help, and he's not very late. I don't see—"

"Dr. Livinski has chosen to end your probation." The teacher thrust back his hood, gold eyes shining down at her. "Good afternoon, Miss Renning."

Aerin's jaw dropped. She tried to stammer out a response, but by the time she had gained control of her tongue, Xioxang had already ducked back in the classroom and closed the door.

Free from work crew! Aerin whirled and sprinted out of the Great Hall. Her boots pounded down the outer steps and quieted as she took off across the mist-shrouded field. She slipped once on the slick grass, but kept running.

Pow! The explosion brought her to a halt like a scarf slung around her neck with intent to kill. She looked up.

Into the venomous stare of Yvonne Entera. The older girl, chin lifted in a straight line, stood less than ten feet away, her feet twelve inches apart, shoulders squared, chest erect. In her hand lay the deep golden handle of a laser, the weapon pointed at Aerin.

Aerin's mind imploded, shattering into fractures of thought and feeling.

"Really," Yvonne sneered, shifting the laser toward a nearby target partially hidden in the mist. "Running across a firing zone is a rather dramatic means of avoiding work." *Pow!* The fire drilled its mark. "Don't you think?"

"I . . . I'm off probation," Aerin sputtered.

"Then why are you in such a hurry to die?" The barrel of the weapon turned back in her direction.

A lump clogged her throat. *Don't let her paralyze you,* she warned herself, taking a step forward. Toward the weapon. "I'm meeting someone."

Yvonne gave a knowing glance at a handful of upperclassmen lurking in the haze. "I don't suppose any of us can figure out who."

There was a spattering of laughter.

Limbs tense, Aerin forced herself to take another step.

"Maybe I should write your parents," the other girl continued. "Warn them about the type of people you spend time with."

Another step.

Yvonne blinked her thick eyelashes. "But then, your parents must have been too busy teaching you combat to stress a little thing like discretion."

Keep walking.

Black eyes narrowed. "He's just using you, you know. Don't think he's actually your *friend.*"

The term stopped Aerin cold. Friend? She was not even sure she knew what that meant. Was it possible that Dane was one? He was not like Yvonne's friends, always hanging around, begging for attention. But she did enjoy his company. She could ask him questions and expect an honest opinion. Was that friendship?

How strange. Hadn't she envied others their friendships, their comfort and confidence in one another? And now?

Now Yvonne Entera envies mine. The thought brought a smile to Aerin's lips and propelled her once again in forward motion. Taking one last step, Aerin closed her hand around the laser in Yvonne's grip, gave it a sharp twist . . .

And wrenched the weapon away.

The episode came back to haunt her the next morning in the cafeteria.

"Did Yvonne Entera threaten you?" Dane's words came from behind Aerin.

She whipped her head around to see him looming over her, his full tray balanced precariously in one hand. There was something in his face, almost—

"Answer me." He took two steps around the edge of the table, and the tray came down with a thud.

"Yes." Of course Yvonne had threatened her. The real question was what had brought this startling reaction out on his face. The Dane she knew did not get upset. He was always controlled.

"Did you turn her in?" he demanded, still standing.

Aerin stirred her food around, then lifted a golden pear off her plate. "You don't honestly expect me to answer that with you glaring at me, do you?" The power of those brown eyes was oddly disturbing.

The pear disappeared. How in the space-time continuum had he managed that? Her reflexes were going rusty.

"Damn it, Aerin, answer me."

Her back straightened. "If you think swearing is going to help, you might as well park that tray somewhere else."

Color flashed through his face: purple.

She was remembering now, what he had said when she asked him why he had broken into the tech lab, something about making bad choices when he was angry. That answer did not seem as evasive as it had before. His thumb was digging a hole in the side of her pear.

"Dane, if you really want to talk about this, let's talk, but stop glaring. You're worse than Xioxang."

The purple faded slightly. "Rumor has it Yvonne aimed a laser at you yesterday."

"Hmm." Aerin held out her palm, waiting for the stolen pear. It returned to her possession.

He sat down slowly. "What was she doing pointing a weapon at you?"

"Threatening me."

"She can be expelled for that."

Aerin frowned. "Don't you dare mention—"

"First-years aren't even allowed near lasers. She should never have had—"

"Dane!" Aerin hissed under her breath. "In case you haven't noticed, I'm not exactly following the rules myself."

"You can't keep secrets like this."

"Why not?" What she said next, she should never have said. She knew better. Their relationship had a wall. She respected it. They both did. But he was chipping away. "It's not like *you* ever share anything you don't want to!"

The purple on his face flared. And she did not dare wait for the explosion. Her body moved—up, around the table, and across the floor. She left the tray with its remnants behind. Her hands hit the exit doors, and her feet pounded down the path.

Halfway to the garden, the déjà vu hit her. *No. Absolutely not. I'm not running.*

The sight of those protective trees reminded her she had been fleeing ever since she left Vizhan. It had to stop. Dane was not the enemy. She had spent enough time with him to know that much. It was time she learned the significance of friendship.

He knew she must have slowed down, or he would have had a far more difficult time catching up with her on the garden path.

"Listen, I'm sorry," Dane said, then cursed himself, remembering how poorly those words had worked in the past. "I don't like seeing my friends in danger." It was an understatement. When he had heard about the threat toward her, only minutes ago and hours after the fact, his blood had flooded his veins, and he had been unable to do anything except explode at the one person who least deserved it.

But she had not told him about the danger. It was frightening how much that scared him.

"You don't need to apologize," she whispered, hugging herself and cracking a faint smile. "I . . . I guess I'm not very good at this yet." She rubbed her arms, then turned and started walking through the garden.

He fell into step beside her. "At what?"

"Friendship." She blushed.

It occurred to him now that his failure to find out from her about the threat might be his fault. He'd been too careful not to ask if she had any problems. Was he so tightly wrapped in his defensive shield, he couldn't see what she was up against?

They walked in silence for several minutes. Then Aerin ducked under a huge cedar branch and stepped off the path. She picked her way through the gnarled trees and overgrown bushes with purpose. Dane followed.

Where was she going? His eyes skipped from the back of her wrinkled collar to the placement of her feet. Maybe she wasn't a classic beauty, but there was something about the way she moved. As if she were one with her surroundings. She crouched and twined her body through the trees without touching them, her hands and wrists curving as though in a dance. How could he have ever thought her plain?

By the time he spotted the pattern of red stones amid the mossy earth, he had lost track of where he was. Sometime, maybe fifty years ago, this had been a real trail.

A light shimmered through the oak and cedar, catching his attention. As he moved closer, the light expanded, then shifted, and he saw that it was not a light at all, but an absence of color. A huge white circle surrounding a stone fountain. She had come here before, he thought, and for some reason, she had chosen to share it with him.

Aerin stepped into the ring. Almost immediately her shoulders dropped, tension sheeting off her face. "The threat from Yvonne," she exhaled, "I didn't mean to hide it from you. I just . . . I dealt with it." She rubbed her fingers.

Belatedly, he realized she had left her coat behind. Though the mist had thinned, there was still a bite to the air, especially with the spray from the fountain drifting toward them. He shrugged out of his jacket, the soft lining sliding easily despite the leather exterior. "What does that mean?"

"I took the laser from her and placed it back on the rack."

As if that would solve anything.

She cocked her head at him, and he had the eerie sensation that she could scan his inner thoughts, witnessing the terror that gripped his throat when he thought of her in danger. "I promise to tell you," she said, "if Yvonne points another weapon at me."

"Or if she threatens you," he said firmly.

There was a pause, and Dane held out his jacket.

She hesitated, then slipped her arms into the lined sleeves.

He folded his own arms around her, pulling the jacket's sides across her chest.

And she jerked away. Like an injured animal out of her depth but prepared to fight. "Listen, Dane, I can't afford to be the subject of an investigation. I don't have anywhere else to go. I don't even know where to hole up for a couple weeks at Christmas. I'm not about to risk my place here just to punish Yvonne Entera." The expression on her face was as determined as Dane had ever seen.

He was about to argue, but the words that came from his mouth were utterly unplanned. "You can come with me . . . for Christmas."

She stared at him.

His eyes dropped, and he kicked at a vine that was trying to invade the pavement.

"Y-you're inviting me to your home?" Her voice held a tremor in it.

Dane tried to push away the images of Chivalry in the winter: the snow, the deep green forests, the frozen waterfalls. They were irrelevant, he told himself. He had to be crazy to think of taking her there. "You don't have to come if you don't want to," he stumbled over his offer. Was he insane? He should back out of this right now.

"Your family?" she asked. "Will they be there?"

"My brother might," he acknowledged reluctantly, both to her and to himself. He kicked again at the vine. "My father is still negotiating with the Trade Union." *Thankfully.*

She flushed, then said, "I would very much like to come."

The attack on the vine ceased. "You would?"

Her laughter bubbled up, the sound bouncing off the white pavement. Startling him. He hadn't heard her laugh before. It was like the fountain, rising up unabashed from the mysterious tangle to a shimmering display.

"Is that such a surprise?" she asked. "Did you think I might prefer hiding out in an alley somewhere?"

He had not thought. Thought had been exempt from the entire proposal. There were about fifty reasons why he should not take her back to Chivalry with him. But in the face of that laugh, well, none of them mattered.

Chapter Thirteen
CHIVALRY FALLS

THE END OF TERM SWEPT DOWN ON DANE LIKE A great horned owl snatching him before he had a chance to escape. Not that he had not thought about it. He had considered and reconsidered his plans to take Aerin to Chivalry, but backing out now would mean letting her down, and he could not do that.

She had changed. It was as if his invitation had unlocked something inside her. The cautious person he was used to finding in the nearest shadow had burst into color. She was laughing and talking and arguing with him in full view of everyone else. He had never seen her look this relaxed. Her cheeks were flushed, and her brown eyes glowed. She waved to him across hallways, walked with him on the way to meals, and waited for him after class. She even smiled when he defeated her for the first time in physical combat, smack in the middle of the term exam.

Dane wondered if she had ever looked forward to anything as much as this trip to Chivalry. He wished *he* could look forward to it.

Dread pulsed just beneath his skin.

Not until he and Aerin had passed their exams, checked out of the dorm rooms, and walked onto the airfield did he feel the first glimmer of anticipation. Pride washed over him at the sight of *Gold Dust*. He ran his hand over the slender spacecraft, then opened the door to show Aerin the black leather seats, multisystem control panel, and six-foot sleeping compartment. "She's an I-36," he said, and broke into a grin. "Handles like lightning."

He could hear his voice begin to yammer: the flexibility of the wing function, the power of the thrusters, the light carriage. *Shut up,* he tried to tell himself. *She doesn't care.*

But her jaw had dropped, as had her single bag of luggage.

He stored the luggage away and offered her a hand up, then leaped into the pilot's seat, anxious to touch the controls. His palms slid over the steering device, and he breathed in the scent of the cockpit. *Imminent flight.* He had not realized how much he had missed it.

One more breath, then he strapped himself in, made a quick check to ensure she was secure, and hit the controls. A dozen panels lit up, and a gentle hum thrummed in the engine. He switched on the radio. "Madousin requesting clearance for takeoff."

"Clearance granted."

His hand clutched the throttle, and *swish! Gold Dust* shot into a near vertical climb. The ship throbbed in the turbulence, then ripped through the atmosphere. A shrill whistle exited Dane's teeth.

And he was once again in open space. How he had missed this.

Aerin said nothing for several minutes. Perhaps she was even more moved than he was. He had not thought about what it must have been like for her, all these months on planet after growing up in the freedom of space.

"How long have you been flying?" she finally asked.

"Since I was twelve." He tossed off the fact, certain she would not care that he had first worked the steering when he was four.

"And who taught you to fly?"

"Pete. He's a mechanic back on base. I've known him forever."

"But didn't your father break all kinds of flight records?" Her voice trailed off.

Why didn't he *teach you?* That was her real question. Dane felt his jaw clench, and instinctively he gave the engine more power. The warning signal started to buzz. *Stupid autopilot.* He switched it off, using the disruption as an excuse not to answer her question. The ship launched into a higher speed, shook for a couple of moments, then smoothed out.

Tension hung in the cockpit. "I can see your instructor failed to impress you with the importance of speed limits." Aerin's voice trembled.

"Oh, well, Pete isn't very impressive." Dane glanced at her, noted the dearth of color in her face, and slowly dialed back the power. "Tell me what you know about Chivalry," he said, trying to distract her from his error in judgment.

She gave a weak groan. "I thought I was done spitting out facts after term exams."

"Don't tell me you haven't done your research," he teased.

She flipped down the star visor, a hint of color returning to her face. "It's a green planet. The vegetation is all natural, unlike most of Academia."

"So what do Academia and Chivalry have in common?"

"They're both circle-of-life planets."

"Which means?"

"The air is breathable." Her normal skin tone had returned. "You know, Dane, I think you're taking this study partner thing too seriously."

He pushed the visor back up. "And why are the circle-of-life planets important?"

"They're ten central planets with natural conditions to support life. The Alliance was built around them."

"Not bad." He clicked his tongue on his front teeth. "And Chivalry's main role in the Alliance is . . . ?"

"It's the central base for the military." She reached for the visor again, then turned on him when his hand stopped her.

"Enough, Dane. I know what the books say. Tell me what your home is really like."

"It's a military base, Aerin"—he spat the words—"not a home."

She bit her lip.

And he wished he had not snapped. He should not allow his own mood to spoil her expectations. There was no reason she could not enjoy her holiday. Or the entire trip, for that matter. If he shared with her, well, if he shared with her what there was on Chivalry to love.

"Know what," he said, his voice softening as a familiar green sphere appeared in the view screen. "I won't tell you about Chivalry; I'll show her to you."

Beautiful, Aerin thought as the green sphere grew larger and larger, closer and closer.

She had read that the military base with its surrounding city took up only a fraction of the planet's surface, the rest being preserved as a wilderness area, but coming from an overcrowded planet like Vizhan, it had been hard for her to believe such a thing.

The reality hit her, though, as *Gold Dust* ripped through the atmosphere, and the spaceship swept into an arc over a vast tangle of leaves, needles, and branches. Shades of green, both deep and light, flickered below, broken here and there by barren branches and the sparkle of silver. The spaceship slowed, and she could see that the silver was a natural shade of tree bark, glowing against the darker browns and reds that filled the inner hue of the forest.

"Almost worth it," she heard Dane whisper under his breath. Then he raised his voice. "Well, what do you think? Better than a textbook?"

She grappled for an answer and settled for the truth. "Beyond words."

Gold Dust skimmed low above the treetops, curving south while Aerin gazed out the window. A deep blue lake shimmered beneath her, the waters stretching in a perfect crescent. Even the forest began to sparkle as they flew over a section where white crystals coated the branches.

Frost, she realized. They had frost here . . . and snow—snow and mountains and forests and lakes. How could Dane have left it? How could he stand to? To exchange this beauty for the stifling Wall of Academy 7. Even space itself lost power in the face of this scenery. The ship was climbing now, scaling the surface of a stunning white slope.

"You ready for this?" Dane asked, fiddling with the controls.

"For what?" Goose bumps spiked her flesh.

"This is Chivalry Ridge. The falls are on the other side."

Falls?

"Hold on."

They were still climbing.

And then they weren't. The land dropped out beneath them, and the plane dropped with it over a thousand feet.

Dane flipped *Gold Dust,* and they were sailing down at a steep angle, the jagged cliff flying past. Aerin dug her hands into her armrests and opened her mouth in a silent scream. *I'm going to die!*

But then she saw the first waterfall, a thin frozen stream of icy blue threading its way down the cliff side, then another one, and another as the plane eased into a curve—a hundred frozen waterfalls sparkling, tracing, and spreading their way across the vertical surface. The sheer beauty broke through her panic. She loosened the mortal grip of her hands.

Dane glanced her way, cracking another smile. "I said to hold on."

And the plane dropped again, this time a sheer fall of about a hundred feet, then plunged forward under the most spectacular vision she had ever seen, the cliff on one side, a frozen arch of ice on the other, a crystal tunnel. Ten feet, twenty. Fifty. Patches of light and dark sprinted over the ship, and she went from blindness to sight a million times in the seconds it took to reach the other side.

Then *Gold Dust* soared away from the cliff's edge before gently curling around and gliding along the frozen falls she had just flown beneath. The exterior glowed, a massive, natural sculpture. Her breath rose and fell with the sparkling light, and she could not speak. What was there to say?

The ship wove its way back and forth, gliding down to a frozen stream deep at the base of the cliff. Then after easing *Gold Dust* onto a small circular landing pad, Dane turned off the power. For minutes, maybe hours, they sat there, Aerin's eyes holding tight to the view.

Her heart thundered in her chest. Could anyone witness such a sight and not have it change them? And what did it tell her about the young man at her side, that he could come from such a place and had chosen to share it with her?

A gush of cold air woke her to the fact that Dane had climbed out of the ship. "Come on," he said, gesturing for her to exit the plane and follow him toward a small, octagonal building at the edge of the landing pad.

She opened her own door and set a tentative foot down onto the layer of snow. To her surprise, the whiteness broke away beneath her boot like nothing. Cold sliced through her leather jacket as though it were made of cotton. She brought down her other foot and hurried after Dane, less concerned about where he was taking her than escaping the chill.

CHIVALRY VISITOR CENTER read the black lettering on the building's glass doorway, and warm air embraced her as she stepped inside. A man in a starched collar came forward as if to greet them, but Dane waved him away, steering her instead toward a drink stand. "Hot chocolate," he told the young man behind the counter, "one plain. One . . ." he glanced at Aerin.

"With caramel," she answered.

The server winked at her and hurried to comply. "Sweet tooth?" he teased.

She blushed but eagerly accepted the warm mug into her

hands. The chocolate slid down her throat in rich ecstasy, and for a moment she was a child again, tasting her father's love.

Dane waited only long enough for her to take that single sip before guiding her through a gap between a pair of painted screens.

She stepped through the space. And froze.

For the eight walls and ceiling of the building were nowhere to be seen. Instead the endless cliff of Chivalry Ridge rose up before them, not as it had moments before, but as it might have done in the springtime. Streams poured in crystal trails down the rock surface; thick moss clung in patches beneath emerald leaves; and the sound of rushing water filled the space, interspersed by the powerful call of a soaring hawk.

The hawk glided down, its wingtips almost grazing Aerin's hair. She reached up a hand toward it, and the bird circled.

Then swept right through her fingers.

She withdrew, flashing her hand front to back for inspection.

Dane laughed. "It's a simulation, created by computer." He stepped forward, dipped his hand into the water at the cliff's base, and returned with a dry palm. "It has sound and three-dimensional form, but no—"

"Substance." She supplied the answer, looking once again at her own hand.

"Exactly. No warmth, no wind, no cold."

She took another sip of her chocolate. "So, it's like a three-dimensional film?"

"Not quite." Dane led her to the edge of the central falls, where shards of surreal spray sprinkled over her face and hands. "A simulator can answer questions and re-create the past without having been there."

"You mean I could ask it how the falls were first made, and it could show me?"

"Yes."

"That's—"

"Genius," a tall woman with a forest green jacket stepped forward. The nametag designating her as a natural history guide peaked out beneath her flat lapel. "Twenty years ago, the Council considered settling the rest of Chivalry, but a young lady brought them here to see her new invention. She convinced them to protect the images they saw in the simulator. Since then, over three hundred thousand new places have been added to the list of protected sites all over the Alliance."

Aerin cocked her head. "If a simulator can answer questions and reproduce the past, why don't we have one at school?"

"It can't be re-created." Both Dane and the guide spoke at once.

The woman turned to face him for the first time, then stopped, staring.

Aerin sighed. How could Dane put up with this everywhere? "What do you mean it can't be re-created?" she urged.

The guide failed to answer, but Dane replied, "The plans could not be found . . . after the designer's death."

"But it's a computer," said Aerin. "Aren't the plans stored in the database?"

Again it was Dane who answered. "Maybe, but no one has managed to retrieve them."

"Can I see the control panel?" The question came out of her mouth without conscious thought. *Don't be a fool. This woman would never let you—*

But the guide was still watching Dane, as if the decision were up to him.

His chin dipped slightly.

"This way, miss," the woman spoke at last.

Aerin did not argue. She followed the guide and Dane back toward the painted screens, then under a black curtain and into a small alcove where, to Aerin's surprise, the woman backed away and dropped the curtain, leaving Dane and Aerin alone with the simulator.

"Go ahead," he said. "See if you can enter the database."

She wrinkled her forehead, wanting to ask what was going on. But not quite willing to risk this chance. Her hands sprang to the keyboard, typed in the Allied entry code, and watched. The machine allowed her in, not even asking for a password, but she soon saw that there was no need for such a tactic.

She had reached only a superficial layer of control. From this section of the computer, she could view images, ask questions, or change settings. But there her ability ended. Every time she tried to probe deeper, a dark gold color flashed across the screen, forcing her back. "It's shielded," she said, turning her gaze once again to Dane.

"Yes," he replied, as though he already knew. "Can you break through it?"

She cocked her head at him. "That's not the point."

"Isn't it?"

"No. If the designer chose to put up shields, she must have had her reasons." Aerin could tell by the way he clenched his jaw that he didn't care. "Dane, did you know this woman, the one who invented the simulator?"

"No." The answer was clipped and wholly inadequate.

Dane blew hot, then cold. She knew that. What she had not known was the startling revelation of the last few hours. How could the person she knew, with his almost constant sarcasm and pessimistic view of reality, come from a place of such beauty? And he felt that beauty. She had seen the look in his eyes, gazing at the frozen falls and their glistening simulated counterpart. She had not known he could feel that deeply. But he had allowed her to see.

And now he was hiding something.

Frustrated, Aerin let her attention drift back to the control panel. Then her eyes caught sight of a name, carved into the metal plaque above the screen. She peered closer, anger bubbling up on her tongue. "Designed by E. Madousin," she read aloud, then turned on Dane. "What does the *E* stand for?"

"Emma," he replied, his voice low. Then it cracked. "My mother."

Dane dropped the curtain behind him and headed blindly out of the visitors' center. Had he lost his mind, bringing Aerin here and dragging her into this mess? *It's not a mess,* his brain argued. How could his memory of his mother be a mess? He had no memory of her. She was dead, had always been dead as far as he was concerned. Death could not be messy. It was life that was. And emotion.

Which was why he should not have come here. He knew better, had known better for years than to put himself in that room with the magnificent falls on the simulated cliff. It was like tumbling off the real thing without a ship.

The sound of boots crunching on the ice told him Aerin had followed.

She did not speak, at least not until they had boarded the plane and had once again taken off. He was grateful for her silence and ungrateful as well. There was something about her, something that made him want to take steps he knew he should not.

She rescued him from his thoughts. "I'm sorry—"

"Don't." What did she have to apologize for?

"I didn't know about your mother," she continued. "I suppose everyone else does."

"It doesn't matter what people know," he replied, keeping his eyes firmly on the view screen. The thick forests were fading, broken by the first scatterings of buildings. "They didn't know *her*. I didn't know her."

"You know who she was. That's something."

Not much.

The buildings began to cluster into the city's outer rim, and Dane checked the speed gauge. He was well under the limit. *You'd think I'd be in a hurry to end this conversation.*

Aerin's next words surprised him, not the statement itself but the fact that she shared it. "I never knew anything about my mother."

He suspected if there was anyone who knew less about his or her own past than he did, it was Aerin. Maybe that was the real reason he had felt drawn to her. Her past was even more of a black hole than his.

"My father never talked about her," she said. "I remember asking him once. The look he gave me—it wasn't happy, or sad. It was more like he couldn't reach me. I never asked again." A catch in Aerin's voice made Dane wonder if she regretted the choice not to press her father for the answer, now that she never could. "I used to imagine he was thinking about her, though, when he would go quiet and stop talking for long stretches at a time. That might sound silly—"

"No." Dane stopped the flow of words. She did not have to explain this to him.

"Your father doesn't talk about your mother either?" she asked.

Not with me.

"She must have been incredible," Aerin whispered, "to build a machine like that."

Dane closed his eyes. For a moment the city disappeared below him, and he could see the hawk soaring again beside the cliff and hear the water pouring over the rocks. He had facts enough about his mother, had read about her. She was a wealthy debutante from another planet, had attended Academy 7, married his father right out of school, and even been asked to join the Council. She had rejected the offer and died young. But none of that, none of that told him anything. It was the simulation of the cliff side with its impenetrable beauty that was all he really knew about her.

He opened his eyes to the stark reality of the military base stretching beneath him. Its shiny black tarmac glittered with frost. His gut gave a sudden urge to flip the plane around, but Dane forced his way past the desire and swept *Gold Dust* into a sharp drop.

Once again, Aerin's hands molded to the arms of her seat. "Shouldn't you radio in your desire to land?"

He shook his head. "Control knows I'm coming."

And *Gold Dust* slid to an abrupt landing. He turned off the plane and removed the strap across his chest. "They've been tracking me since I entered the atmosphere."

"Tracking?"

"Aerin, this is a military planet." He shoved open his door, climbing down backward in order to keep talking. "They track every vehicle in Chivalry airspace."

Especially mine. He opened the side luggage compartment, then froze.

There was no warning. No sound, not a footstep, but suddenly he knew. The knowledge came screaming over him. *Count from ten,* he ordered himself. *Ten, nine, eight . . . You're fine. You're fine. You're fine.*

And he turned to face the rigid glare of General Madousin.

Chapter Fourteen
CHRISTMAS

AERIN FOUND HERSELF LOOKING OUT THE PASSENGER doorway into the deepest pair of blue eyes she had ever seen.

"Leave it to my brother," said the owner of the eyes, "to make a lady wait." A smooth, pale hand opened itself in front of her chest in a gesture of expectation.

And she took it. Within a moment she found herself swept forward, lifted close against the dark fabric of an air force jacket, and set down softly upon the ground. It happened so fast she did not even have a chance to cringe.

The tall young man standing before her laughed at her shocked expression. He tucked a lock of blond hair behind his ear and lifted his strong jaw. "Paul Madousin," he introduced himself. "And you are?"

Heat spread its way up her cheeks as she answered, "Aerin Renning."

"A pleasure to meet you." Paul took a slow step back. "I'm sure my father will agree." He cradled her arm just below the elbow and guided her around the tail of the plane.

His father?

She almost tripped as she saw the older version of the young man she had just met. The eyes were the same blue, the skin the same pale shade, the jawline just as strong. His stance emanated strength, as did the chest sporting its row of polished medals. He was a full foot taller than his youngest son, and nearly five inches taller than the young man still guiding her arm.

"Aerin, this is my father, General Gregory Madousin." Paul dropped his head in a gesture of respect toward the older man. "Father, this is Aerin Renning."

The General's hand twitched. Then his thumb hooked under his chin, and his finger stroked the side of his nose. When the hand came down, a smile spread across his face. Aerin had imagined Dane's father as stern and strict. The smile belied that assumption. "Miss Renning?" He repeated her last name carefully.

"Y-yes, sir," she stammered.

He offered her his arm. "It appears my youngest son has some sense after all. May I escort you to our land vehicle?"

Aerin broke the gaze, seeking out Dane. What did he think of his father's surprise appearance? Her classmate slouched against the hood of the silver vehicle, his arms folded over his chest. He was watching his father, not her.

Unsure what else to do, she took the arm of the most powerful man in the universe and climbed into the vehicle with its tinted windows, two rows of facing seats, and a white curtain that separated the passenger space from the driver. Paul seated himself across from her, General Madousin at her side. Dane crawled in last, slamming the door.

She tried to catch his gaze, but he slumped in the seat opposite his father and fixed his eyes on the ceiling.

"I apologize if I showed a lack of grace at your reception, Miss Renning," the general stated. "I'm certain I would have done better had I been aware of your coming."

Aerin blushed. "I . . . I am sorry, sir," she said. "Dane and I were under the impression you were still negotiating with the Trade Union. I hope my being here is not a problem."

The older man smiled. "Nonsense, my dear. This family could only benefit from a female presence." The general paused, then gave a wink and explained, "The negotiations were halted until the end of the holiday. Sometimes even the Trade Union is easier to communicate with than my youngest son." The comment made her uncomfortable, but Dane did nothing to negate it. He continued staring at the ceiling.

"Tell us, Aerin," Paul said, "what convinced you to spend your vacation here?"

The questions carried them along, Aerin finding herself without any choice but to answer. Dane did not once open his mouth. Annoyance grew within her at his sullen mood, but his brother and father made her feel so welcome that she was at ease in their presence by the time the vehicle pulled to a halt. Dane exited the vehicle without a glance in her direction, but Paul offered her his arm and whispered in her ear, "Welcome to our home, Miss Renning."

She stared in shock. Marble walls stretched up before her: three, four, five stories high. Polished steel trim curled its way around dozens of windows as well as a set of double doors at the center of a huge, glass-enclosed patio. Silver wreaths circled the door knockers, and silver vines twined around columns every fifteen feet. Couldn't Dane have mentioned that he lived in a mansion? No, perhaps not. Perhaps she would not have understood. Like with the falls.

A thin woman in a gray kerchief pulled open the doors, and Aerin stepped into the endless patio. Midnight-blue glass formed three distant walls, and an obsidian floor swirled with traces of silver and gold. It was like standing in empty space, as though someone had tried to remake it and almost succeeded.

A sudden softness brushed her cheek. From across the patio, Dane sent his brother a sharp glare. Paul ignored the look and winked at her, then pointed up at a strand of mistletoe. Embarrassment flooded her face as she realized the softness had been his lips upon her skin. Had she entered some alternate reality?

By the time she went to bed that night under a canopy

of golden silk, she was certain of it. Her first walk through the house had been filled with one miracle after another: the pine logs burning off their scent in the fireplace, the fir tree dressed in a cascade of tinsel; the vanilla candles lining the piano, buffet, and wide dining room table. And Dane had said this was not a home. It was more magnificent than anything Aerin had ever imagined in her childhood fantasies.

Enticement woke her in the morning, the scent of warm muffins seeping under her covers and luring her to the breakfast table. Dane sat alone, mopping the crumbs from his plate. "Thought we'd fly to the Southern Rim today," he said, wiping off his fingers on one of two thick coats hanging at the back of his chair.

Glad he was talking again, she retrieved a muffin from the basket and poured herself a full mug of hot chocolate before sitting down. "The Southern Rim?"

"It's at the edge of an ocean. The storms there are spectacular this time of year."

"Is it dangerous?"

He grinned. "Only slightly."

A warm bite slid down Aerin's throat. She had no desire to leave this place in exchange for danger. "When would we go?"

"Go where?" a slurred voice came from the doorway. Paul entered the room wearing nothing but a pair of pajama bottoms and fuzzy slippers. The muscles on his chest gleamed under the overhead light.

Aerin felt her mouth go dry. It took her several seconds to realize no one had answered the question. "The Southern Rim," she blurted.

"Ah." Paul eased into the empty chair and gave a meaningful glance at his brother. "That's an all-day trip."

"No kidding," Dane replied.

"Is that a problem?" Aerin asked. She reached for the butter at the same time as his brother. Instead of pulling away, Paul captured her hand.

Porcelain thudded against wood on the opposite side of the table.

Blue eyes held her attention. "It's just that our father will be disappointed to be deprived of your company," said Paul, "as will I." He turned her fingers over and kissed her palm.

Chair legs scraped across the polished floor.

She had not thought how it might appear, her taking Dane away from his family on his first day of vacation. "Maybe we should wait a few days," she told the blue eyes, "rather than leaving so soon."

"No!" Dane stood with such force the table vibrated, and chocolate spilled from her mug. Aerin rushed to sop up the liquid in her napkin, then cringed as the brown stain seeped into the fine cloth. She looked up apologetically.

Both brothers were eyeing each other: Paul seated in his chair, calm face unreadable; Dane standing, shoulders tight, chest about to explode. She felt like a stranger from another dimension, coming upon an argument she did not have the skill to interpret. Then, without explanation, Dane grabbed the coats from his chair and stormed from the room.

Her gaze flew to Paul, who just shrugged a bare shoulder and opened the honey jar.

With a reluctant glance at the remaining chocolate, she snatched a muffin and ran after her classmate, catching up to him at the sliding-glass door to the patio. "What is the matter with you?" she demanded, feeling her patience thin. "Your brother and father have been nothing but polite to me. You would think I was *their* guest instead of yours."

Dane braced his hands on the edges of the doorway and stared down at the obsidian floor. "I'm sorry, Aerin. I shouldn't have put you in this position."

"What position?" She could feel her exasperation building.

"In between." He slipped his arms into one of the coats and strode out on the patio, leaving her more confused than she had been before.

Then he turned. "I'd like to take you to the Southern Rim today . . . if you don't mind."

What could she do? She could not mend the rift between him and his family. And it was becoming clear that any attempt to do so on her part would spoil her friendship with him. "What should I bring?" she asked.

"Yourself." He tossed her the other coat. "And this."

Aerin had never seen anything like the Southern Rim. White-crested waves shattered over pointed stone formations. Thick swaths of fog draped the distance, obliterating the horizon. Spray came up from below, and rain threatened from above. Water filled the world.

At least it seemed to from Aerin's viewpoint behind the giant wall-length window of the visitors' deck. Dane deposited her on a huge white cushion by the window and brought her a cup of steaming chocolate. "To make up for this morning." He grinned.

She took a sip, her eyes widening as the sweet taste of caramel eased down her throat. He had remembered her request from the day before. She cocked her head and studied Dane as he settled down at her feet, his eyes watching the waves crash below. There was so much she had not known about him, back at school. His regard for beauty. His attention to detail.

And there was so much she still did not understand: his hostile behavior toward his brother and father, the intensity of his reaction when she had witnessed his mother's name, his infatuation with the violent scene below.

"Doesn't it frighten you?" Aerin asked as a fierce gust of spray hammered the window.

"That's why I like it," he said, his hand sliding close to hers. "The early explorers on Chivalry, they thought if they found the right material, they could make a ship to withstand her wild seas. They tried everything: steel, ironite, Maravan gold."

She raised her eyebrows. Maravan gold was even stronger and more costly than ironite. "They failed?"

"Miserably," he said, and pointed out at the giant stone formations, then toward the side of the room. "You see what those rocks can do to metal when it crashes against them at the speed of a Chivalian wind. That's a remnant of a ship."

She stared at the mangled hunk of metal threaded along the edge of the visitors' deck. Gaping holes punctured the metal's center, and long silver strands wrapped around the edges, bending back and forth on one another. She had thought the metal was a sculpture, perhaps an abstract version of the sea. There was nothing left of the battered shape to define it as a vessel. "And you find that fascinating?"

"Yes."

She thought about all the times she had envied Dane his bravery. When he had argued the controversial side of a heated debate topic or climbed the scaffolding without a ladder. And yesterday, plummeting his plane over the edge of a cliff to soar through a tunnel of ice. There *was* something enviable about his total lack of fear. And disturbing.

She glanced again at the shredded metal that had once been a ship. "Why?" she asked. "Why is danger so appealing to you?"

He didn't look at her, his gaze turning back to the window where the sky had opened up to a bolt of lightning. His hand closed over hers as she shuddered. "I'm not sure," he whispered, "but sooner or later, those waves—they'll defeat the rocks."

*   *   *

The intimacy that had defined their journey disappeared immediately upon their return to the mansion. General Madousin, clearly upset that his son had chosen to spend the day away from home, had held up the evening meal, an act Aerin found hard to understand when Dane declined to speak a single word to his father. It fell to Paul to ease his father's hurt feelings and keep the conversation going.

The same pattern filled the following days. Aerin and Dane would spend the daylight hours exploring the natural wonders of the planet. In the evenings, they would return to the mansion, where he would slip into silence.

A pattern that did not break until Christmas.

That morning Aerin arrived at the breakfast table to find a stunning emerald green necklace coiled on the center of her plate. General Madousin draped the extravagant gift around her neck and secured the catch. She saw Dane's jaw tighten. Did he not want her to receive the gift?

In contrast, Paul swept her a deep bow.

She blushed with shame at having nothing to give in return, but the general ignored her apologies, then directed both her and his sons to the base chapel, where they attended a religious service and watched a special performance of singing, music, and candle lighting by local youth.

Upon the return to the house, the general suggested everyone retire to prepare for a formal dinner at two o'clock. Wondering how the others could require an hour to prepare for a meal, Aerin climbed the stairs to her bedroom slowly.

The sight that greeted her there caught her by complete surprise. A red velvet dress with golden trim hung from the bed's canopy. She drew close, fingering the soft cloth. Embroidered in the lace along the neck were the figures of birds: doves and nightingales, each one unique. Never in her life had she touched anything half so fine.

Afraid the dress might not fit, Aerin tugged off her clothes and unhooked the gown. She slipped under the skirt, eased the neckline over her head, and slid her arms into the long sleeves. The soft fabric smoothed down over her skin without a wrinkle. Her mouth opened as she stepped in front of the mirror. The bodice fit perfectly, hugging her waist and chest, hiding the scars on her shoulder, and the skirt flowed long enough to cover her school boots.

The hour almost flew as she tried to make the rest of herself suitable for such a gown. She bathed, then dressed once again and seated herself at the vanity, struggling to do something with her long hair. Her fingers had no skill, and she finally gave up, settling for brushing out the strands until they hung down her back in simplicity.

Before she knew it, the hour hand on the clock pointed at the two. Gripping her skirt in each hand, Aerin eased down the stairs and made her way toward the dining room.

Her entrance met with stunned silence. Neither Dane nor General Madousin said a word. They both stared as if a foreign presence had entered the room. Dane's face went pale, and his eyes glowed a deep, intense brown.

It was Paul who rescued her, leaping from his seat to offer his hand and escort her to her chair. "Very effective," he whispered in her ear.

The lights had been dimmed, and every one of the vanilla candles in the room was lit. At the center of the formal dining table sat a huge roasted turkey, dripping with orange basting sauce, and bowls of creamed potatoes, fruit sauces, and salads were scattered across the lace tablecloth. Bread loaves covered by silver fabric rested in a basket, and a trio of serving maids stood in the corner, each waiting to refill any emptied glass or platter.

General Madousin bowed his head to give grace. Then the plates began to shuffle, and Paul, who sat on Aerin's right, told her the names of rare dishes, offering his own advice on which to take. The table conversation began with talk about the performance at the chapel, then drifted into the topic of advanced schooling, and finally, to Aerin's discomfort, settled upon her.

"How long have you attended Academy 7, Miss Renning?" the general asked.

"I started this year," she replied, lifting a spoonful of tangy cherry sauce to her lips.

"And where were you before that?" The general took a sip of wine.

Her spoon wavered. *It's a natural question,* she told herself.

He has no reason to suspect I'm not a citizen. But this man, perhaps more than any other person, enforced the laws of the Alliance.

"I . . ." Aerin fell back on the story she had given Dane. "My father flew a trade ship, and I traveled with him until he died."

"I see." General Madousin's voice held a strange note in it, measured but compelling. "And your father's name?"

She found herself answering with honesty, though her voice shook. "Antony was his real name. Most people called him Tony."

The wineglass hit the table.

"When did you say your father died?" This time the question came with abrupt speed.

Aerin felt her heart lurch. She had not said. She did not want to lie to this man. But she could not answer the questions that were bound to follow if she told him the truth. "R-recently."

Dane rescued her, speaking to his father for the first time throughout the entire visit. "Perhaps we might leave that topic for a less-painful one."

The older man gave his son a long look, as if weighing options. A slow nod signaled his choice. "Well, Dane, you could share your impressions of my alma mater instead."

For an instant Aerin worried that her classmate might abandon the conversation, but he did not. Instead, a halting dialogue arose between father and youngest son.

"It's a challenge," said Dane.

"Glad to hear that hasn't changed." The general wiped his lips with his embroidered napkin. "And which part do you find the most challenging?"

"Living up to your reputation." Dane's mouth creased in an ironic twist so that it was impossible to tell whether he was mocking his father or telling the truth.

The general chose to believe the latter. "I believe I still hold a number of records there."

Dane spun his glass in a circle. "Which would you say is the greatest?"

The general launched into a story about his shooting prowess. Aerin tried to catch her classmate's eye. Judging by the stacks of plaques and trophies she and Dane had rescued from corrosion, the records of past students were not that greatly valued at Academy 7. It was kind of Dane to bring up his father's achievements.

"And that," the general said, winding up his story, "was the last time an older student bragged about having the best aim on campus."

"First-years aren't allowed to shoot anymore," Aerin said.

"Hmph," the older man replied. "That's Jane for you, making rulings that undermine the integrity of the Alliance."

Jane?

Dane answered Aerin's unspoken question. "I believe Dr. Livinski feels students should first have a firm foundation in the more traditional forms of combat."

The general scoffed. "And what have you wasted your time on this year?"

"He earned the second highest mark in physical combat," said Aerin, jumping at the chance to improve her friend's status in his father's eyes.

"Second?" The general arched an eyebrow.

"You'd be surprised at the competition." Dane met Aerin's gaze, threatening to bring the conversation back to her.

Quickly she withdrew from speaking, letting herself enjoy the silent role of observer. The glasses clinked and drained and filled again. The desserts came forward, chocolate cubes in pools of cream. And Dane and his father talked. Perhaps now the tension between them would ease. Surely, whatever had strained their relationship would not last in such a magical place.

She could not sleep that evening, not even under the golden coverlet and ruffled canopy. The memory of the special day had wrapped its way around her mind and proceeded to run in smooth clockwork circles. As it wound through a third revolution, she finally gave up, flung back her covers, and retrieved her empty water glass from the bedside table. Time for a mission.

The sound of voices coming from downstairs distracted her. She must not, then, be the only one having a hard time letting this day slip into the past. Careful not to trip in the dark, she crept downward. A dim light came from the patio, and she could make out two shadows on the other side of the tinted glass, but as she reached the lower floor, her steps slowed. The tone of the voices was far from pleasant.

"What did you think you were going to achieve, bringing her here?" the general demanded.

Aerin froze, realizing he was talking about her.

"I thought I might enjoy the vacation," answered Dane.

"Don't sidestep me." The general's voice rose as the larger shadow neared the smaller one. Standing close to his son like that, General Madousin's massive height and extra bulk were apparent. "You and I both know that isn't why she's here."

"Do we?"

"Until this evening," said the general, "I assumed bringing her here was your idea alone."

"It *was* my idea. I invited—"

"Stop!" The shout cut through the glass. "Just stop pretending. I knew you were baiting me with that dress."

"The . . . the dress?" Dane stuttered.

"Don't pretend you don't know where it came from. You must have broken into your mother's room." The accusation pierced Aerin's mind.

"I had never seen that dress until today," said Dane.

Somehow Aerin knew he spoke the truth. The young man who had flown her past those waterfalls would never betray his mother's memory, not for something as crude as spite, no matter what his father believed. Had the red velvet belonged to Emma Madousin? Aerin eased toward the open gap in the patio's sliding-glass door. Perhaps she should apologize, explain how she had come to wear the dress and how she had never meant any disrespect. But if neither the general nor Dane had left the gown, who had?

The response came from Dane, only a few feet away now but still oblivious to her presence. His back and shoulders were rigid. "I don't suppose it occurred to you," he said to his father, "that my brother might have taken the dress."

"What interest could your brother have in an urchin like that?" The general's words were like a slap. And suddenly Aerin did not want to be there, did not want to hear where this was leading. But she could not move.

She could see clearly now through the opening. The general was facing her, but at an angle, his attention fully taken up by his son. Anger rimmed his face in rough lines.

"Oh, I'm sure Paul has no interest in Aerin," said Dane, "but he would like nothing better than to have you accuse me."

"Don't blame this on your brother!"

"How could I? Nothing's ever his fault."

"This isn't about him."

"What is it about?"

"Aerin *Renning*!" The general growled out her last name. "You will remove her from this house by noon tomorrow."

"What am I supposed to tell her?" Dane's response shook. "That my father has lost his mind and wants her gone."

The fury in the general's voice dropped to a frightening

calm. "Tell her the truth. I caught her in that lie tonight at dinner, and you rushed to cover her tracks. You were in on this together, throwing it up in my face."

The water glass fell from Aerin's hand.

Dane took a step forward, toward his father. "I . . . do not . . . know what . . . you are talking about."

And in that instant General Madousin shot out his fist and hammered the side of his son's face. Aerin jumped in horror.

Dane had doubled over, his hands clutching his cheek.

"Go to hell," the general said, his voice as low as it had been before the sudden attack.

"I'd be glad to leave you in it," Dane replied, stumbling to the opening.

And then he was there, staring at Aerin, blocking her from the general's view. His hands dropped from his face, and she could see the brilliant red mark across the top of his cheekbone. Without a word, he gripped her shoulders, turned her around toward the stairs, and pushed.

She could hear the glass slide shut behind her.

Chapter Fifteen
PAIN

DANE WOKE UP TO PAIN ON THE COLD PATIO FLOOR. His left side screamed, far worse than the burning cheekbone under his eye. He struggled to lift himself off the obsidian and felt the darkness tilt around him.

Fire scorched through his torso, and something slid.

The jarring memories from the night before slammed into his conscious. He should have known better than to fight back. Two months of Aerin's unorthodox training could hardly outweigh a lifetime. Dane had known he didn't stand a chance.

There was no blood. Too sloppy. Not the General's style.

Somehow Dane picked himself up off the floor. He stumbled through the opening in the glass, then sank against the wall.

Stairs.

He considered not climbing them, turning instead and walking away, never coming back.

But he could not leave Aerin behind. One hideous, bone-jarring step at a time, he made his way up the staircase. After the second step, a foggy gray haze settled over everything, and he stopped thinking about the movement, just kept going. An amazing thing, pain. Like a drug, massacring thought.

At the top, he banged on the outside of her door and called, "Aerin, we're leaving." He did not bother to return to his room. There was nothing there worth the agony of carrying. "Aerin!"

She appeared in the doorway, her bag in her hands, concern blaring across her face.

He could not talk to her, could not think about what she had seen. Not right now. She was a shadow at the edge of his peripheral vision, a necessary attachment and nothing more.

Boxes were waiting for him on the driveway: ten, maybe fifteen. All labeled with his name on them, the General's way of kicking him out of the mansion. Dane ignored them. No thought or emotion went into dealing with those boxes. He could only walk around them, cross the barren cement, and head for the airport.

He had to walk. No way would he beg a ride from his father's chauffeur.

The pain provided his only sustenance. He felt stripped, as

though every soul on base were watching him. The only defense he could muster was to keep his head lowered, averting his eyes from stares. He thanked the pain for its welcome haze.

A haze that splintered when he spotted the gray hair, greasy coveralls, and familiar face waiting for him by the tail of the plane. *Pete.* Dane felt everything inside him break, like a million branches cracking under the torrent of a windstorm.

"Been avoiding me?" the mechanic accused.

With a trembling gesture, Dane motioned for Aerin to board the plane.

She frowned, her gaze centering on the older man, but she followed directions, shoving her bag into the storage compartment and climbing into the passenger seat.

Pete watched her shut the door, then turned toward Dane. His head shook with an odd, wobbly rhythm that made him look older than his age. "You knew this would happen," he said.

Dane did not bother to ask what. Pete just knew, the same way he always knew and was always there to pick up the pieces.

"You can't afford to keep coming back," the older man said. "Your father is never going to change. He'll destroy you."

Dane blinked. Pete was never this blunt, never came out and actually stated the truth about the General, at least he never had before.

"Or he'll find an easier target," the older man added, dipping his head toward the passenger side of the plane.

"He didn't hurt her," Dane rushed to say. *He's never hit anyone but me.*

"He might. If he thought it would get to you."

The words were the same ones that had hammered through Dane's brain last night when he had heard Aerin drop the glass. And he had experienced real fear, the type he had thought he was oblivious to. Immune. But his immunity had failed.

"He's never getting another chance, Pete." Dane choked. "I'm not coming back."

The older man didn't protest, just held out a callused palm. This, then, was why he had come to the airport.

And for the first time, Dane knew why he, himself, had returned to Chivalry. And why he'd invited Aerin against his better judgment. Not because she wanted to come. That had been the excuse. The truth was he had needed her, needed someone to validate his own actions, to stand at his shoulder and distract him from the fact that he was never going to see this planet again.

Not the dense, raw beauty of its wilderness or the simulated spectacle of his mother's legacy. Or the weathered face of the man in front of him. For an endless minute, Dane stared at the tarmac, trying to gather control. Then he forced himself to meet the gaze of his closest friend and slowly took the offered hand in a firm grip, to say good-bye.

Chapter Sixteen
DENIAL

HE SHOULD NOT BE HERE, AERIN THOUGHT AS SHE stepped onto the academy field and peered at Dane through the deluge of pouring rain. She could not blame him for not speaking to her in the week since their return to the school—that is, she could, but she probably would have done the same thing in his situation. And she could not blame him for keeping to his room and leaving her to fend for herself on the almost deserted campus. Nor did she fault him for attending this morning's classes on the first official day back. She understood that, too. But this, this was idiocy.

Miss Maya may have given the entire first-year class an hour's reprieve from the rain with her lecture on second-semester expectations, but she had been very clear that no such respite would be available during combat. "You must learn to fight under any conditions" had been her mantra since the beginning of the damp season. And now with the driving raindrops rebounding off the pavement and slamming into the grass, Aerin knew she was about to face the true meaning of that statement.

She had never fought in the mud before, nor in anything worse than a steady drizzle. There would be problems, pitfalls she should be worried about. Techniques she should be contemplating.

On another day, the prospect of fighting in the downpour might have consumed all her attention. But Dane's stupidity was making that impossible.

He has no right to be here.

Miss Maya, looking more comfortable in the torrent than she had in the overcrowded classroom, brought her silver whistle to her lips. It gave a shrill shriek as she gestured for the students to team up. "All right, let's see who wants to stay at this school!" she shouted through the rain.

Aerin glared at Dane as he shuffled in front of her and settled his feet into opening position. What did he think? That she didn't know he could barely walk. He hadn't been to a doctor. If he had, Miss Maya would never have let him on the field. It wasn't fair—his putting Aerin in this position.

Once again the whistle blew.

He didn't attack.

Not surprising for someone who can't even carry his own luggage. She doubted he could block, much less perform an assault. And if he was counting on her to attack first, he could forget it.

She did not move.

He waited, and she could see the comprehension dawning slowly on his face, a shadow replacing delusion. She could hear the other students around them launching into maneuvers, flinging one another upon the sopping ground, prying their bodies out of the mud.

He closed his eyelids and took a stutter step back.

Aerin did not speak. She did not have to.

Because Miss Maya was standing over them now, her keen stare taking in the uneven step and the ugly, mottled bruise on Dane's cheek. She stepped forward, between him and Aerin, then placed hands on her hips. "Madousin," the teacher ordered, "take yourself straight to the nurse."

Still Aerin did not move. She watched him go until there was nothing left to see but the thick curtain of pounding rain. And the fierce reflection of betrayal in his eyes.

She managed not to think about him for the rest of the afternoon. Shutting herself down. Focusing on the skills required not to kill herself or her reassigned partner. Afterward, she took a shower, buried herself in her studies, then rushed off to the cafeteria. Alone.

But there, her careful avoidance fell apart.

"Can you believe they let him stay?" a snotty female voice carried down the almost empty table.

"Of course they did," came a second voice. "He's Maya's favorite."

Aerin shot a quick glance toward the two speakers, recognizing them both as fellow first-years: a short dark girl with a penchant for copying off others' papers and an athletic blonde whose work was not worth copying.

"Ha!" the dark girl scoffed, twining her spoon between her slender fingers. "Do you think if one of us was roughed up in a brawl over vacation, we'd still be here?"

A brawl? Was that what they were calling it? Well, the gossip mill would have had to come up with some explanation for the bruise on Dane's cheek, and knowing him, he would not have discouraged the rumor. He may have started it.

"Hardly," replied the blonde. "He's lucky to get away with just three cracked ribs."

Aerin winced. Three cracked ribs! How could he consider going to class that way?

"It's because of his father," the blonde continued. "Anyone else, and they'd have been thrown out with a thud. That's probably the only reason he got accepted in the first place."

Aerin felt the blood run down her tongue before she realized she had bitten it. She knew Dane would not want her to defend him. Watching him today had been like seeing him self-destruct.

Still, these girls had no right to speculate.

"That's not true," Aerin found herself interrupting. "Dane is one of the best students in the school. He doesn't need any special favors."

Two sour looks turned her way. "Oh really?" said the blonde. "He's getting a two-month reprieve from physical training, and that doesn't sound like a special favor to you?"

"What are you?" the dark girl added. "His girlfriend?"

"I doubt it," smirked her friend. "Did you see the look he gave her when she humiliated him in class today?"

"Deadly."

"Besides"—the blonde pointed across the room—"could he be sitting any farther away from her?"

Aerin's head flew up. Sure enough, Dane was at the far corner the room. For an instant his head came up and his gaze met hers, then turned away without acknowledgment.

She began sawing at a potato skin with her knife. If he wanted to punish her for refusing to let him kill himself in physical combat, that was fine. She could live with that. He could ignore her all he wanted. She had always expected him to lose interest in her. Slowly, however, the force behind her knife lessened.

If she were honest with herself, truly honest, then she should admit . . .

That she had begun to think of her friendship with Dane as more than temporary.

That she understood why he had walked into that deluge this afternoon.

And that the wall of separation that had grown between them this week was her fault. He had built it to replace the one Aerin had torn down. She had seen what she was not supposed to see, and he could not forgive her, because the balance of secrecy had tipped, the scale sliding too far in her direction.

She knew that. She understood.

And she knew how to end it.

The only way to repair the damage was to rebalance the scale by spilling her own darkness into the hole she had made in their friendship.

But she could not do it. It was out of the question.

Some secrets were too painful to share.

Chapter Seventeen
THE NIGHT

EVERY NIGHT THE NIGHTMARE CAME. FOR FIVE months. Dane tried to ignore it. He tried to eliminate it by applying himself to his studies and filling his brain with all manner of knowledge. He pushed his body to the edge, first in rehabilitation, then in training, hoping to exhaust himself, to make it impossible to dream.

It did not work. *When you have the same dream over and over again, your brain is trying to solve a problem,* Pete always said. *It knows there's an answer.*

If there were answers in Dane's nightmare, they had yet to reveal themselves. He awoke the final evening of the school year as always, sweat pouring down his skin, his mind determined once again to live and relive his last argument with his father. *Lucky,* the school nurse had said. *If the fellow had punched you any harder, you would be dead.* Luck had nothing to do with it. If the General had wanted to puncture a lung, he would have, and he would not have cracked the ribs if he had not wanted to.

But Dane had been the one to inflict the deepest damage. He had chosen to sever his relationship with Aerin. Because he had not been able to face her, could not accept the fact that she had seen him at his weakest and most vulnerable.

Again Dane struggled with the memory of her standing outside the sliding-glass door. Watching.

He thrust the image away and rolled over, picturing her instead in the red dress. Was that what had sent the General over the edge? The dress? That had been Paul, enacting his revenge for Dane's entrance into the school.

Paul had never been able to stand being beaten by his younger brother. And it had happened before. Often enough that Dane had learned to recognize the pattern, and repercussions, at an early age. The General would blow up, blasting out accusations, and somehow Dane was always at the center of the blast. But his brother was the fuse.

This time, though, there had been more to the fight than Paul. *I caught her in that lie tonight at dinner,* the General had said, *and you rushed to cover her tracks.*

What lie? Dane had rescued Aerin from his father's prying when the General had asked about her past. But what was the lie he thought he had discovered? And why would Aerin's secrets about her personal life matter to Dane's father? It was

almost midnight when a thought took Dane in a new direction. His father had been probing Aerin at dinner. Looking
for personal details, but his questions had not turned
demanding until she had told him her own father's name.
Tony. No, Antony. Antony Renning.

Dane had seen that name before.

He sat up, shoving off the sheets. After tugging on a pair
of pants, slippers, and a shirt, he hurried into the hallway. He
had to talk to Aerin. Now.

She was not in her room. He became convinced of that fact
only after banging on her door and waking up half the girl's
wing. By the time he realized that she must have sneaked
out her window, the wing monitor on night duty had arrived
on the scene: Yvonne, still fully dressed in her uniform, an
expensive watch, and a green necklace.

Reminiscent of the one his father had secured around
Aerin's neck at Christmas, strangling Dane as he fastened
the brass catch. He'd wanted to rip the false jewels off her
neck, to accuse his father and brother of using her to get
to him. Flaunting their power through her naivety. But he
hadn't known how to warn her of their insincerity without
frightening her.

It was yourself you were protecting. Admit it, his conscience
taunted him.

Hell yes, he'd been protecting his own secret. And it had
almost cost him everything.

"Problem?" Yvonne asked, arching a tweezed eyebrow.

"No." He hedged away from Aerin's door, his brain clicking rapidly, hunting for a way to explain himself and keep Aerin off Yvonne's radar. "I must have been sleepwalking." He gave a sheepish grin. "Sorry."

The exotic girl bestowed him with her version of a placating look, an expression that reminded him of a feigning predator. She slipped an arm around his shoulders and ushered him back up the hall. "You're sleepwalking in the wrong wing," she teased, then, instead of escorting him back to his room, she stopped at the staircase. "Would you like to go down for some hot cider?"

No. But the drink machine was on the first floor, and that would put him almost where he did want to be: outside looking for Aerin. He nodded.

Yvonne let him open the door for her.

They started down the steps. She kept glancing at him as though expecting him to say something. "Nervous about tomorrow?" she finally asked.

He wrinkled his forehead, then realized she must be talking about the morning's ceremony when the names of the returning students would be announced to the universe. He wished nerves were all that was keeping him awake. They were a good enough excuse. "I guess," he replied.

She traced a violet fingernail over his wrist. "I would have thought you of all people wouldn't be worried. Your marks are even better than mine." A hint of bitterness rifled her voice. "Yours and that . . . Heron-girl's."

Dane squelched a desire to correct Aerin's name. He had reached the bottom of the steps. The lobby stood before him, with the front door a mere ten feet away. "You know, Yvonne." He tried to detach her fingers. "I think some fresh air might be better for me than cider."

She giggled, linking her arms around his waist and facing him. "You know I'm on duty, and it's after curfew."

"I just think it might help get my mind off things a little." He reined in the urge to pull away and lowered his voice in the name of a greater cause. "Maybe by the time I come back, you won't be . . . on duty."

"Be back by two," she whispered in his ear, then let go.

That was one appointment he would not mind missing. Three smooth strides and he was out the door, closing it firmly behind him.

Night had turned the garden into a forest like something from a dark fantasy. Dane garnered scratches and bruises as he picked his way through the shadows. A sickly sweetness clung heavy in the air, the chaotic blend of rampant, untended flowers. His eardrums were invaded by the high-pitched cry of tuneless crickets, eventually replaced by the *shhh* of running water.

He found Aerin in a pool of moonlight by the fountain. Tree branches reached out their fingers toward her slender body; but the light seemed to emanate from her, pushing them away. Her back faced him; her long brown hair split down the middle and swept forward across her left shoulder; her thin arms bent at the elbows.

She is beautiful. The thought slipped into his conscious as it had once before, when he had first seen her in the red dress. Suddenly the discovery that had brought him here felt less urgent. He needed to repair the damage he had done first, to explain himself and apologize. She deserved that much.

"I never meant to place you in danger," he said, stepping forward from the shadows.

Her shoulders straightened, but she failed to turn.

"I didn't know my father would be there," he added. "I would never— I should never . . ."

"Your father didn't touch *me.*" Her words wavered.

He swallowed. This was hard, harder than anything he had ever done. "The General started hitting me when I was nine. He said . . ." Dane swallowed and struggled to keep his voice. "He said it was because I was a coward."

A strained sound between a laugh and a sob came from her. "So now you aren't afraid of anything?"

Unease crept over Dane's shoulders. That was the idea, but it wasn't reality. He had been trained never to show fear, never to admit it. "I was afraid of you," he told her, "of what it meant to have you *know.*"

There was a long, long silence. And just when he thought they might never surpass it, she spoke. "I'm the reason your father was angry. That night, he was upset because of me."

"Don't." Anger stifled Dane's voice. Had his rejection made

her think he blamed her? "He's like a time bomb, Aerin. The same thing would have happened with or without you there. I just . . . I couldn't talk about it . . . what happened that night. It had nothing to do with you," he rushed to say.

She was shaking her head. "Yes, it did, Dane. Maybe you're right about your father. If I hadn't been there, something else might have set him off, but that night it was me. It was what I said at dinner. Your father, he wanted to know when my father died, but I couldn't tell him. I was afraid if your father knew, he would want to know where I was after my father's death, before . . . before I came here. I don't . . . I don't know how he knew—"

"That you were lying." The misshapen piece began to slip into place, and Dane felt a sudden rush of betrayal.

"I didn't intend to lie."

It was still a lie. She had been lying to him all this time. And she knew the deepest, most unforgivable secret Dane had. "Where were you then?" he asked, no longer willing to respect her privacy. "If you weren't on a trade ship?"

She caught her breath. He could see the muscles tighten in her neck. There was another long silence, and then she said, "My father died in that ship seven years ago."

Dane stared, not certain what to think.

"In a crash," she finished the thought. "I was with him."

Instinctively he reached out a hand to touch her shoulder.

She yanked away. "The computer . . . it malfunctioned. My father was trying to take us to the next space station, but it was days off; and I couldn't fly without the autopilot. I was trying to fix the processor."

"Seven years ago? But you would only have been—

"Nearly eleven years old." Her hand ran through her hair. "I've always had a gift with technology, but not enough of one. The ship went down and crashed."

"I thought you said you were days away—"

"From the nearest space station, but not the nearest planet. We landed on Vizhan." The name tilted off her tongue, jostling through his memory.

His brain leafed through the stacks of material he had studied over the past months. "Vizhan?" he repeated.

And then he remembered what little he knew. *A minor X-level planet in the Dyan sector of the universe, ruled by a small group of people who subject the majority of the planet's inhabitants to slavery and sporadic culling.*

Culling? The word bit into his gut. What was that? A polite word for murder?

She stared into the fountain's sheeting curtain. "I don't remember much from right after the crash. I saw my father's body and . . . I guess I was in shock. There were people. I don't remember them trying to talk to me. They were more concerned with the ship. It was a long time before I realized they didn't know what it was."

"The ship?"

"Vizhan is isolated. The people there have no concept of flight."

His throat rejected the notion. He knew there were planets outside the Alliance that had lost scientific knowledge, but still, if the planet was inhabited by human life, the people must have come there by ship originally. "No concept at all?" he asked.

She shook her head. "I think the leaders must have rebelled against space travel at some point, though the man who owned the property where we crashed, he kept my father's ship, even though he didn't know what to do with it—left it like a monument in the field where it landed. He collected things: land, machines, people."

Dane's hands clenched into fists. "You were a slave?" he asked.

She paused. A shadow traced its way across her back. Then the words began spilling from her throat as if she could no longer contain them. "I was housed in a shed with over a hundred people. The smell . . . it was like death. There wasn't enough food. You had to fight."

That was how she had learned the skills she used in combat and why she talked about them as if they were a matter of survival. Understanding slid into Dane's mind.

"We were herded to work in the fields," she said, "flat-open areas where only a few guards with weapons could control dozens of people. The guards . . . they would stand up on platforms. If we were too slow, or made a mistake, or they just didn't need us anymore, they would fire their lasers."

Bile rose in Dane's throat. His hands lifted to her upper arms, and this time she did not pull away.

"One day"—Aerin's voice had gone sandpaper harsh—"the owner pulled me off field duty to fix an ancient computer. He had a lab filled with them, but they were almost all dead. He must have thought I might know something, considering all the machines on the ship. I fixed it, the computer. And nearly all his other ones. It kept me out of the fields a few days a week. In three years, through trial and error, I made everything in that house run by machine: the lights, the doors, the running water. Then there was only one computer left in need of repair. I stalled on it for months. Until the day he lost his temper."

Dane's hands tightened on her arms.

She reached up, covering his left hand with her palm, and pried his fingers away, then undid the top buttons of her uniform and eased the fabric over her shoulder. To reveal the dark lines of an X burned into her skin. "He branded me."

Dane's body jolted. He could not accept that X and the pain it told him she had endured. It rivaled anything his father had ever done to him. Physically.

"That night"—she took a deep breath—"instead of returning me to the shed, he locked me in the lab." Her voice hardened. "That was his mistake. As soon as it was dark, I sabotaged his security system, shut it all down and let myself out. There was a forest running from the owner's house to the field with the ship. The trees gave me cover. I never would have made it without them."

Tension ran under Dane's skin. *But the ship had been damaged before the crash. What if she hadn't been able to fix it?*

"Hardly anything wasn't damaged," she said as if reading his mind. "I'd learned a lot in the lab, and I managed to fix the autopilot and part of the control system, but if the ship had failed . . ."

She turned toward him, silent tears streaming down her cheeks. And then she was trembling, sobs escaping her throat. He knew now what she had done. A runaway slave committing sabotage and theft. A suicide mission really. Pinning her life on the chance, no matter how slight, of escape. No wonder she lived in fear, jumping at danger. No wonder she questioned her safety in the Alliance. No wonder she judged and doubted people without letting them close. He wrapped his arms around her and pressed her to his chest in a fierce embrace.

"Aerin." She heard Dane say her name through a thick down of cloudy memory. "What do you know about your father? I mean about his past—where he grew up, his family?"

"I don't have any family." She spoke into his shirt.

Dane began to pull away, and she didn't want him to go, didn't want to lose that strange, unreal feeling. Of safety.

But the firm hands slid from her back, and the warm cocoon withdrew as he insisted on talking. "Your father must have had family though, at some point. He must have come from somewhere."

She shivered, trying to wipe away the tears that blocked her vision. "I don't know. I'd give anything to know more about him."

Dane swam into view, a blurry figure blending with the darkness. "Then there's something I need to show you." He reached out for her hand and pulled.

She found herself following him with an odd sense of detachment. Too shaken emotionally to think about much, she focused on his steps. He plowed ahead recklessly, willing her forward through the garden and across the grass.

Not until he pulled a pair of lock picks from his pocket did she bother to wonder why he was taking her away from the dorm.

"You remember that conversation at Christmas dinner?" He paused at the foot of the Great Hall.

Hadn't she just admitted it had haunted her for months?

He scaled the sloping steps, then looked down at her. "You said you didn't know how my father knew you were lying."

She eyed him with a frown. "It was almost as if—"

"He knew when your father died."

She froze, unable to react as Dane slid a small tool into the keyhole of the main door. His fingers moved with deft ease. *Click, click, click* came the response. And then the massive door was opening. He pushed it in and gestured for her to enter. She shook her head in refusal.

He hurried back down to her, placed his hand beneath her elbow, and guided her easily with him.

The hallway was dark. Too dark to see after the bright moonlight of the outside, but Dane did not wait for her eyes to adjust. "Stay here," he said, then sprang up the stairs.

"No." She tried to stop him, but he disappeared in the blackness. The sound of creaking steps rose farther and farther above her, echoing in the high space.

She fell back against the wall. What was she doing? Once before she had sat in this building alone, in that empty basement room, the terror of the dark ripping apart her sanity. And that instance, too, had been Dane's fault. At the time, she would never have believed she would risk her place at the school. Yet here she was, putting herself in the same situation she had been falsely accused of eight months ago, and Dane had not even given her a real reason. What had changed in her world that she could accept this?

Everything. Everything had changed.

And nothing.

"Aerin." He was standing before her again. By now her eyes had adjusted, and she could see him. The light from the window played across his features: strong cheekbones, dark hair curling behind his ears, eyes shining with anticipation. He stepped closer. "You remember that day when Dr. Livinski made us clean the trophy room?"

She remembered all too well. The punishment she would receive for this night's excursion would be far worse.

"Xioxang handed me a plaque," Dane kept talking. "He ordered me to clean it. I wouldn't have even looked at the thing, but it had my father's name on it: Flight Team: Gold."

Her patience had worn out. "Your father won a million awards." She pushed off the wall and turned to leave.

"He did." Dane blocked her path. In his hand was a rectangular piece of polished wood. "But every flight team has two members."

"I don't care if there are fifty members. The announcement ceremony is tomorrow, and if Dr. Livinski finds us here, neither one of us will be on a flight team. Ever."

"Aerin, there's another name on this plaque."

She waited.

"Antony Renning."

The name reverberated off her eardrums. It flew up along the stairway, repeating and repeating and repeating until it rebounded off the ceiling and entered her soul.

"My father?" she whispered.

Dane held out the plaque.

She took it, pulling the slick, carved surface up against the window's light. And read her father's name.

"How?" Her hands began to tremble. "How do we know it's him?"

"It would explain a lot," Dane replied, "about the General's reaction to you. If he knew who your father was, he might have thought I brought you home as some kind of ploy. And he might have known when your father died."

"How could—"

"Don't forget who my father is, Aerin. He has access to data that never reaches the public, and even if he doesn't know about the crash, he could still know when your father disappeared."

She felt a flood of emotion: anger at Dane's father for what he might know and had not told her, doubt that any of this could be real, and hope—ridiculous, stupid, breathtaking hope. Her words came out in a firm question. "How do we find out?"

Dane gestured toward the basement. "We look. That is, if you can break through Zaniels's new clearance program."

She met his gaze.

He needed no other reply.

Within moments they stood in pitch darkness outside the tech lab. There was another series of clicks as Dane worked at the lock beneath the keypad; then the door slid open. Ivory light glowed from the machines. The room's soft hum beckoned her in.

And a louder whirr vibrated as she flicked on Zaniels's computer. Golden light spread across the screen. Her fingers moved, interrupting the loading process and bypassing the clearance program.

"If your father was a student here, his records should be in the archives," Dane said. "At the very least, there should be a picture you can use to identify him."

With Dane's advice, she began the search, entering the

restricted school files, then the archives. A white box popped up, asking for a name.

Her fingers typed in the letters, A-N-T-O-N-Y-R-E-N-N-I-N-G.

Swish! Colors flashed across the screen as the machine rifled through its memory. A pause. Then a basic directory appeared with links for grades, awards, and postgraduate data.

Beneath them emerged a simple school photo of a student, a young man with black eyes. A cowlick kicked up his dark hair just to the left of his forehead. Unmarred skin covered his cheekbones and jaw. His mouth spread in an irrepressible grin. So unlike the man she had known. And yet it was him. Her father.

Aerin stared, soaking in the view of that face. Alive. Uninjured. A picture to replace her last haunting image.

"It's him, then?" Dane asked, shifting his stance and bringing her back to the present.

"It's him." For the second time that evening, saltwater stained her vision. Her father. *Here.* In the Alliance. Her heart stuttered as she took in the implications. He was a citizen then. And according to Allied law, so was she. Was it possible?

Yes. In fact, knowing what she did now about the security at Academy 7, it was the only real explanation for why she had been accepted here with her real name, and why she had never been exposed as an imposter. Because she wasn't one. She had just as much legal right to be here as anyone else.

Aerin blinked, gathering herself and calming her emotions. But if her father had grown up here, why had he never spoken about the Alliance? And why had he left? She slid the cursor toward the first heading on the page.

His grades sprang onto the screen.

"Doesn't look like you inherited all your strengths from him," Dane said, pointing at a row of C's for tech analysis.

"No." She gestured at another C for combat. "But he had one of your weaknesses."

"I," growled Dane, "have an A in combat."

"You wouldn't if I was teaching it."

"Well, there's a reason you're not." Dane slid his hand toward a row of A's under introduction to flight. "Looks like he was destined to be a pilot."

"Maybe," came her response as she moved on to the awards page.

"Definitely." A list of flying awards covered the top of the screen. "Best in Class, Pilot: Rank 1, Air Strategist," Dane read some of the titles aloud. "You'd think he was the one in line for the rank of military general instead of my father."

"I guess they had something in common," she whispered.

"I'll say," Dane replied. "Wonder if they were rivals."

"And flight team members?" she asked with doubt. She scrolled down the page, this time reading aloud herself. "Best First-Year Essay: Planet Rebellion. Best Second-Year Essay: Flaws in the Alliance. Best Third-Year Essay: Allied Failure."

"Ouch!" Dane murmured. "Guess we know why he didn't make military general."

"Second Speaker: Debate Team. Universe Debate Champion."

"Jeez, Aerin, your father knew how to argue."

She glared at Dane but couldn't keep a smile from spreading across her face. This was a new feeling, sharing pride in her father with someone else. She moved on to the final award on the list. "Graduation Speaker."

"Not bad," Dane teased.

She sat down in the chair beside the computer and clicked the heading for post-graduate data.

A sullen blank screen met her request.

She waited but nothing appeared, and her chest began to feel hollow.

Dane must have been disappointed as well. "Try a more general search," he urged.

"I've done that before," she said. "Nothing comes up. He's not famous like your father."

"Try it here. Maybe there's something else in the private data bank for the academy, something that's not under student files."

She followed his directions, doubt warring with hope as she produced a new search box. Again she typed in her father's name. Again color lit the screen as the computer searched and searched and searched. Aerin glanced up at the glowing clock, 1:06 A.M. She turned back to the screen.

And the blood left her face. The name, Antony Renning, had appeared, not once but again and again, all the way down the screen. Her trembling hand scrolled down the list of sites for almost a minute.

Dane let out a low whistle.

She clicked on a link. Sheer blackness covered the screen, and they waited; but as with the postgraduate data, nothing came up.

Aerin returned to the list and chose another site. Again, darkness.

She pulled a strand of brown hair between her teeth and chewed on the end as site after site produced the same reaction.

Dane's palm closed over her right hand. "Aerin, look at the screen." Her eyes moved once more over the page with the list of her father's name. "Read the descriptions next to the sites."

She had overlooked the small white font. It had seemed irrelevant with the lure of news about her father only a click away, but now the writing gripped her, not only for its content but because it was all the same.

Slowly she scrolled down the list. Each address was different. They were all different sites, all different places with some tie to Antony Renning. And next to every heading, in that small white font, was the same single word. *Classified*.

Chapter Eighteen
FLIGHT

CLASSIFIED. THE TERM SCORCHED THE INNER LINING of Dane's brain, but his eyes focused on Aerin. It was her word. Her barricade.

Which did not explain the look on her face. Those set eyebrows and pursed lips implied more than frustration and more than the type of thought required to cover her tracks as she exited the computer.

A twinge of fear crept up Dane's spine.

She shoved in her chair and left the lab.

"Aerin!" Dane swept one last glance around the room to make sure it was the same as when they'd entered. He scrambled to lock the door, then hurried after her.

She had already made her way down the outer stairs by the time he reached them.

He jumped the steps and landed before her. "Tell me," he demanded.

Clouds had drifted in, covering one of the moons, but the light remained strong enough to highlight the determined look on her face. "I need to find answers."

"To what?"

"Whatever the Council is hiding." She set out across the grass.

"Where are you going?" He was not sure he wanted to know.

She stopped. And looked up. Over the roof of the Great Hall. Above the solid black wall encircling the grounds. To where the clouds themselves drifted around the spinning coils of the dark tower.

"No!" His gut responded. When had she started listening to rumors? "You don't even know what's up there."

"The Center for Allied Intelligence."

"You don't know that."

"But you do, don't you, Dane!" She whirled to confront him. "Being the son of a Council member must be good for something."

"That's not fair." *True. But unfair.*

"If there's classified data about my father, it has to be stored on a computer somewhere. And what better place than in that tower? Which just happens to be on the grounds of a school run by a Council member. And the Spindle just happened to be built right after Dr. Livinski joined the Council."

Aerin and her research. "You don't know what you're risking." He tried to reason with her. "If someone caught you hacking into that material, they could charge you with espionage, and that's only if you survived the trip." He pointed at the black coils turning in the air. "That tube is the only entrance to the Spindle. It moves counterclockwise which means the pilot has to fly into the rotation. And the slope shifts. Some of the best pilots in the universe couldn't make that flight."

"You could."

"No."

"Then I'll go myself." She set out in the direction of the airfield.

"Damn it, Aerin, you don't have a plane!" He followed.

"I'll take yours."

"The hell you will!" He grabbed her arm.

She spun to confront him, her hair lashing his face. "You started this, Dane. You're the one who craves danger. Why are you so scared now?!"

Emotions crashed over him. He had been building up to this forever. Since she had knocked him on his backside that first day in combat. He should have figured it out when he had practically torn his way out of lockdown at the thought of her under arrest or when he had exploded with anger after Yvonne had threatened her. But he hadn't understood. Not even when he'd wanted to plaster his brother to the wall after Paul had lured her beneath the mistletoe.

Not until she'd walked through the door in that red

dress. Her bare skin dropping to the low neckline, red velvet streaming down her arms, her chest, her waist—and flowing in waves to the floor. It had terrified him, not her beauty, but his sudden, urgent desire to pull her to him. Because he had known then that this relationship had gone further than he had ever intended. Beyond his control. Though he had tried for months to deny it—to deny the inevitability of this moment.

He kissed her. For one single, frozen instant his lips were on hers, begging her to understand. That his fear came from needing her. It was the danger to her life that frightened him.

Then she slapped him, giving a sharp cry, as if she were the one who had been struck. "I don't need someone to tell me *no*."

Her rejection rammed into his chest with harsh intensity. If he had stopped to think, he would have known she was not ready for the kiss. Her heart was still barricaded by her father's death. But at that moment Dane knew he had lost. Not only the battle with his own will, but the argument. She had laid down the gauntlet, and he had every right to be afraid.

He could feel fate tightening its claws as he crept through the airfield. The humidity had grown heavy, and the clouds had continued to build, blocking out the remaining moonlight. It was dark, too dark.

Thud! Aerin swore. "Sorry," she whispered, doubling the error.

He maneuvered her behind him and continued forward. Her hand settled on his back, pushing him or trying to calm her own nerves through human touch, perhaps both. But he was not about to be pushed. The planes would all have their own alarm systems.

He inched his way along, past outthrust tails and tilted wings. Twice he ducked to avoid equipment not seen until almost too late, and once he pulled Aerin up close to save her from banging her head on an exhaust pipe.

Gold Dust was at the rear of the lot, where it had been parked for the past two terms. He wound his way around the battered training vehicles used for second- and third-year students, then skirted a handful of more expensive machines that he assumed belonged to academy staff members.

Finally, he spotted the smooth curve of his own craft. Aerin's hand dropped from his back, and within minutes they had both boarded the plane. Dane leaned his forehead against the control panel. The tension refused to drain.

He felt none of the rush that usually accompanied him in an act of defiance. He could lose his license for this, not to mention his freedom and education. But that was not what bothered him. It was the knowledge that he was not alone. One slip. One miscue up there, and she would die right alongside him.

His hand hovered above the controls. He knew this next

step was the most dangerous in terms of getting caught. Though *Gold Dust* had a soft engine, the initial start-up would cause a momentary burst of sound before sliding into its low hum. "Are you certain about this?" he asked Aerin, keeping his voice soft. "You could still opt out." *Attend the morning ceremony without fear of rejection.*

"I can't," her voice rasped.

He understood, though he wished at the depth of his soul that he did not.

"Start the engine, Dane."

He complied. The control panels lit up, and sound roared in his ears. The hair on the backs of his hands rose.

Get up! Get up! his mind screamed, urging him to take off before anyone in hearing distance had a chance to track them down. He reigned in the panic, forcing himself to scan the radar for overhead movement. Nothing.

And he lifted off.

Vertically. With no lights.

Every muscle in his trained body argued that this was unsafe, but he could not risk running the lights this low to the ground. He plastered his gaze to the radar. It remained clear.

The altitude reading scaled up. A thousand feet. Two thousand. Three.

That was his cue. The headlights beamed into focus, and his hand shot forward, switching to manual. He tilted the ship.

The lowest point of the Spindle's long black tube whipped around just above the plane and raced off on another circuit. Darkness camouflaged the remaining spiral, but Dane knew that eight full coils stretched above him. A marathon.

For now, though, only the opening mattered. *It's all about the angle,* he told himself, positioning the plane. *The angle and the speed.*

Aerin gasped as the entrance neared once again, moving at seventy miles per hour.

He didn't look at her, didn't want to see the doubt on her face. It was too late. The headlights were a beacon to anyone peering up from the ground below. He needed to enter the spiral. And he needed to enter now.

Now!

He hit the throttle, and the rotating tube engulfed him. White seam lines split the darkness. *Use them,* Dane ordered himself. *They're there for definition.*

Blood thundered in his chest, and the pumping sound grew faster and faster as he soared upward. *Stay strong,* he commanded himself. *Steady.* The edges of the steering device bit into his hands. His foot refused to lift. There was no air, none that he could feel. No lungs. No breath.

Only the sucking spinning coils of white seam lines and darkness. He gave himself up to them. Nothing existed beyond those coils. Not Aerin. Not the school. Not his father.

Dane melded with the plane. His eyes were the windshield,

his hands the controls, his heart the engine, beating and beating and beating its way to the top.

The coils grew steeper, shifting the flight pattern. And now there were more lines. Red this time and running crosswise. Not guiding. Distracting. Jumping at him. Flashing past. Thrum. Thrum. Thrum. Trying to drag him under.

Dane filtered out the red. What if the white seams, too, began to mislead? What if they also detoured or faded to nothing?

Where was he? In the fifth coil? The sixth?

Don't think. Fly.

And now the tube was narrowing. A centimeter at a time. Drawing closer and closer to the edge of the wings. One hitch. One jerk in the flight path, and the plane would hit, bounce off the spiral in a pounding ricochet, and bathe in a shower of flames.

He had been insane to try this. Insane to think he had the skill.

And then the seams were gone! The red. The white. Momentum carried him forward into the black tube of certain death.

Chapter Nineteen
THE SPINDLE

THEN LIGHT.

An open cone of light.

Gold Dust soared into the empty cavity. The ship swung up in a steep arch, drained itself of speed, and dipped down in slow descent, once again a machine, a separate entity. Hovering in the air. Not able to land.

Dane examined the open room. The black stem of the Spindle rose up through the center. A flat ceiling stretched above him, and a matching white wall slanted its way from the ceiling's circular edges down to a point at the bottom.

He scanned the sloping surface. Smooth. Except for a single ridge. *There!* A welded seam sweeping horizontally around the cone. As he focused, he could just make out a shift of light and a flat, glass surface—the landing pad.

Gently he eased *Gold Dust* down, released the landing gear, and felt the slight rock of the ship as it came to rest. He pried his grip from the steering device, then lifted his hands to gaze with wonder at the blood oozing down his palms.

Aerin stared. The blood was like a dagger, one more slice in what she had thought she knew about Dane, and hadn't. She had pushed him into this flight, leveled it at him because she thought he could not resist the challenge. From the ground, the spiral had been just a curling design on a structure to her, a decorative obstacle in the path of what she wanted and thought she needed. Her desires.

Her gut had sucked in when she saw the spinning tube up close, but she still had not really understood the danger.

Until that ride. Not a trip through a moving tube of black material, not for her. It had been a living, burning memory. Not of a moving spiral, but of a spiraling crash in another ship six years before. With another pilot. One whom she trusted and relied upon. One with far more experience than the young man she had pushed into flying this night.

And the blood at the end of that crash had been deadly.

Far worse than the pair of crimson lines drizzling down the palms of the friend at her side. Or was Dane more than a friend? *His kiss:* she had not known how to react—had known only the sudden, sharp fear of uncertainty.

She should say something, thank Dane or apologize, but

her tongue felt weighed down, unable to form the words. Instead, she ripped two swaths of lining from the inside of her uniform and wrapped each of his palms in the fabric, tying a secure knot on the back of each hand.

With the second knot, her tongue returned. "We won't go back."

"What?" Dane spoke as though in a daze. She wondered what horror had lived in his mind on the journey here.

"We won't fly back on our own. We'll radio someone and ask for help. I'll tell them the truth. It was my idea. I never would have—should never have asked you to do this for me."

He pulled his hand away abruptly. "We're here now. Let's find what you need."

He exited the ship, and a moment later, Aerin stood on the floor of clear glass. She looked down at the point below her with the black stem running through it.

Dane was moving now in a slow circle around the landing pad. "This is only the hangar. The records must be kept on another floor. There should be an entrance somewhere."

Aerin set off in the opposite direction, her nerves shivering. She scanned the white wall for the slightest crack, but nothing interrupted the smooth ivory flow.

"In the center," Dane said, as he met her on the other side of the room, "there's a keyboard."

She approached the vertical cylinder. A small section of the stem was divided into panels, all black without letters or numbers; but they were, as Dane had said, in the shape of a keyboard.

She bit her lower lip. This was no simple machine. Aerin knew all computers had an override, built in by the maker in case of needed repairs, but it was one thing to find the override on a normal computer. If she failed, she could always shut off the machine and try again. There might be no second chance with this keyboard, and judging by the deadly spiral, the consequences if she failed might be fatal.

Her fingers trembled as she typed in the entry code, *Alliance.* A curved screen of white light lit up on the stem just above the keyboard. Before she had time to try a basic command, a maze of letters and numbers began to shift across the screen. *A map,* she thought. These were the steps, if she could figure out how to read them. There! Amid the maze, the letter J sped across the screen in a straight diagonal. She hit the key where the J should be. Then the letter A in the same formation. The letter N. She hit them both. E.

And all the other letters and numbers swirled down in a tornado toward the bottom of the screen where they disappeared. A simple question replaced them followed by a blinking cursor, "Up or down?"

Aerin turned to Dane. What could be down? They could see the Spindle's bottom point.

"And I thought this was going to be hard," he said with a grin.

Her forehead creased as she typed in the term, "Up."

Zzzzh. Beside the keyboard, a crack split and widened

within the black stem. An opening, eight feet high and two feet across, revealed the hollow inside of a tube.

She heard Dane catch his breath. Thin white seams edged the stem's interior in two long vertical lines. Down. All the way down into nothingness.

Aerin crouched low, placing her hand on the glass surface of the landing pad. She slid her palm forward into the hollow stem. Her fingers glided over a crack, then moved forward. Solid. "More glass," she whispered. Carefully she stepped inside the stem. "It's an elevator."

Dane showed no sign of joining her. He was still staring at those thin white seams. Fearing she might be left alone, Aerin grabbed him by the elbow and yanked him into the stem. A second later, the door closed, sealing itself. Once again, they had entered a hollow tube, someone's nightmarish creation. Aerin felt Dane's hands circle her waist.

Tilting back her head, she could see the top of the stem. The distance was hard to judge, perhaps a hundred feet. Then the surface beneath her shoes gave a slight shudder, and she was moving. The distance began to shrink. Now ninety feet. Now eighty. Seventy. Dane's chin bit into her collarbone, and his arms pressed tight to her rib cage.

A second shudder brought the movement to a halt, and again the crack opened, revealing yet another vast white room, a mirror image of the first.

She stumbled forward, thankful to escape the narrow stem and grateful to stand on the solid white floor. The tentlike wall stretched up to the Spindle's topmost point, the slanted surface once again smooth.

And empty. Aerin felt a lump lodge in her windpipe as she searched for anything that might store information. She skirted the outer wall and the stem. Nothing. Not even another keypad.

This she realized as the door slid shut.

"We were wrong." She felt her legs waver as hope drained from her body. "It's not a Center for Intelligence."

Dane steadied her. "No one went through the trouble of building this tower to hold nothing."

"It's a prison."

"I don't think so," he replied. "There are speakers in the floor." He stooped down and ran a hand along the surface.

She crouched beside him and felt the tiny ridges grouped together.

He backed away toward the outer rim of the room and peered up at the top. "Along the ridge of the stem." He pointed. "Those are light fixtures."

"Lights and speakers." She could hear her voice shake. "Of what use are they in finding answers?"

Now Dane met her gaze, a shine in his eyes. "It's a simulator."

She swept another glance around the room. "I thought there was only one."

He smiled. "This makes two."

"How do we . . . how do we turn it on without a key-board?"

Dane raised his voice, no longer speaking to her. "Simulator, data request."

"Access code, please," an electronic voice responded with clarity.

Dane looked at Aerin, and she looked back at him. How could either of them ever guess the access code? *An override?* she mouthed to him without speaking.

He shook his head, slipped his fingers through the strands of his hair, and rested his palms at the back of his skull. She saw his chest rise and fall. Then his chin came up and he spoke. "Emma."

There was a pause, a slight *whirr*, and an answer. "Access code confirmed. Awaiting data request."

Aerin's mouth opened, then closed. *Of course, the access code was the name of the woman who had designed the first simulator and no doubt this one as well.*

"Awaiting data request." The computer repeated.

Dane gestured toward Aerin. This was her mission, her quest.

"Antony Renning," she said, letting her voice echo off the white walls.

"One hundred files available. Limit search."

Limit search? How was she to do that? She wanted to know everything about her father. But she might not have much time. She had to begin with her most vital questions. "Why did he leave the Alliance?"

There was a soft *whirr*. Dane slipped to her side as the room went dark. And the simulation began.

Chapter Twenty
SIMULATION

SHOUTING INVADED THE DARKNESS. AERIN FELT Dane go rigid and pull away as she recognized his father's voice. "I can't believe you, Tony. You're a traitor!"

"And you're a sellout, Gregory Madousin! I thought you wanted to save the universe."

Her heart exploded at the sound of the second speaker's voice. Seven years she had been trying to shut herself off from the memory of that voice, from the memory of the man who had raised her and loved her and left her behind in hell when his ship had crashed. The man whose death had severed her heart into fragments and almost destroyed her.

And now her father's image solidified: his narrow shoulders, the swath of dark hair, and those gray eyes shot through with specks of green. It was him.

And yet not him. For both he and the man squaring off across from him looked younger than she had ever seen them, barely older than Dane or her.

The entire scene felt eerie. Black chairs, matching lamps, and a pair of footstools emerged, all clearly those of the Academy 7 dorm lobby. And in the background, two vaguely familiar female figures lingered on a brown sofa.

But Aerin had no time to try to identify the young women. Her focus, like theirs, hinged upon the argument between her father and the future general.

"After all the Alliance has given us," the young version of Gregory argued, "the education and the skills." He flung up a pair of skinny arms that had yet to catch up with his tall frame. "You want to disregard all that!"

"I'm not betraying my education," replied Aerin's father. "I want to put my beliefs into action."

What beliefs? The man she remembered had always been kind, but she could not recall his employing that trait in the name of anything larger than her welfare.

"You can do that within the Alliance, Tony. Join the fleet."

"And follow orders like you? Not likely."

A shade of red climbed up above Gregory's collar. "It's an honor to fly for the Alliance."

Her father stepped back a single pace. "I'm not saying it's not." He took a breath. "It's just not for me, not how I want to make a difference."

A brief silence descended, and then a female voice broke into the lull. "Where will you go, Tony?" One of the young women slid off the couch and seemed to float rather than walk as she came forward to stand beside Gregory. Her black hair coiled around her head in a formal manner, and her slender arms rested with ease at her sides.

"I thought I'd start with Mindowan," Tony answered. "It's not far from the Alliance, and its citizens will understand the concept of freedom even if they've never experienced it."

Mindowan, Aerin had heard that name before, in debate class, by Yvonne, of all people, stating that the Alliance could not afford to lose another trade partner like Mindowan.

The woman tilted her head. "It's a monarchy, isn't it? With a king."

"And a princess waiting to inherit. The people have absolutely no say in their government."

"Then they haven't asked for one," Gregory grumbled.

"Haven't fought for one, you mean," Tony argued. "The Council refuses to help them because Mindowan is a vital trade partner. It's one of the only planets in the region willing to sell ironite to the Alliance. And oh, the Council would never want to disrupt its best interests."

A stab of familiar pain twisted in Aerin's gut, the same pain she had felt upon learning of the Alliance's hands-off policy with regard to X-level planets.

"Mindowan is a peaceful planet in the middle of a violent sector," growled Gregory.

"And that's one of the reasons I'm going there. I want to effect peaceful protest, not violence."

"I know you've never been loyal to the Alliance, but I thought you would at least stay loyal to us." Gregory swept a hand to include the two young women. "We've been friends for years; at least I thought we were."

Tony pursed his lips. "I'm not betraying us, and I don't believe I'm betraying the Alliance. Sometimes you have to break the law to live out the values of the Manifest."

Gregory's head vibrated. "The Council won't see it that way."

"We understand what you're saying, Tony," said the young woman at Gregory's shoulder. "None of us think the Alliance is perfect. And what you want to do, help liberate people on nonmember planets, it's an admirable goal."

"But he could do it through the Alliance!" Gregory snarled.

"Not on Mindowan," said Tony, "or any other planet labeled off-limits. Someone has to help those people." His face had tightened, sharp lines running through his brow, his chin jutting in determination. Aerin had never seen her father this way before, flush with passion. Had he truly been like this once?

"You may be right," said the woman, "but you know if you succeed, Tony, if you incite rebellion on these planets, the Council will denounce you. They can't afford to anger other governments."

"That's why I have to go, Emma, because the Council won't."

Emma? Aerin's gaze shot back to the young woman. She stood out like a relief against the future general at her side. Where he was pale, she was dark. Where he was angry, she was calm. She slipped her slender hand into Gregory's, and now Aerin knew why this woman looked familiar. Because she had passed those same dark eyes and hair on to her son.

For the first time during the simulation, Aerin spared a glance for Dane. His eyes gleamed too bright, and she knew the sight of his mother had affected him much as her father's image had affected her. Dane had gone paler than Aerin had ever seen him, the color fading from his lips.

And then the simulation, too, began to fade. Her heart twisted as her father disappeared. She closed her eyes, struggling to imprint every moment of the past few minutes into her brain.

Then the irony struck. Seven years she had pushed away the memories of her father, and now she clung to one that was not even her own. The moments stretched as she grappled with that reality.

Dane's words broke the silence. "Well . . . now we know what happened between your father and mine."

"They were friends," she managed to say.

"Close ones, or my father would never have been so angry with yours for betraying the Alliance."

"You think my father did it, then, left to start a rebellion on a foreign planet?"

"That was what you asked the simulator, wasn't it? To explain why your father left the Alliance?"

She had forgotten about her initial question. "Yes." Aerin struggled to take in her father's actions. His motives, of course, had been noble, but how could he risk all the blessings of the Alliance? A chill ran through her limbs. "And do you think my father was denounced by the Alliance, like your mother said?"

Dane brushed the back of his hand over one of his eyes. "It would explain why your father never came back."

And why he never talked about the Alliance. Or Academy 7. Or anyone from that time in his life.

But it did not explain why her father had changed. Why he had lost the passion she had just witnessed and stopped fighting for his beliefs. Why he had exchanged those dreams for months in isolation on a trade ship with only his daughter for company. Or why he had a daughter at all.

And then Aerin knew what question to ask next. It had nothing to do with the Alliance, nothing to do with revolution or politics or what was legal or illegal. It was the question she had asked only once and thought she would never be able to ask again. The unanswered question that had haunted her life long before debate class, or Academy 7, or even Vizhan. "Simulator," she said, "who was my mother?"

Before she had a chance to second-guess herself or wonder how the computer could hope to identify her, much less her mother, the *whirr* of the machine commenced. And once again the simulation began with voices.

"What if we lose?" questioned a man.

"Yeah!" hollered another. "What if we're arrested? I've a family at home that'll be thrown out in the streets if I can't work."

"I've seen that place of yours, George," said a third. "I don't reckon the streets would be much worse."

Images began to form. A diverse crowd in a cobblestoned square gathered around a podium. Men, most of them in rags, pushed their way toward the center, their voices piling one upon another. A second group of men, these in clean breeches and fitted jackets, looked on with curiosity, and a sprinkling of women, some toting children on wide hips, scattered the crowd's edges.

Aerin peered at the women, searching for one who could be her mother, but her father's voice distracted her.

"Listen, I'm not here to tell you what's best for you or your families." His words came from the podium. "I can't promise you safety or freedom. But I can tell you your one chance to change Mindowan is to work as a group." Gone was her father's school uniform and the short haircut he had worn in the last simulation. He was dressed like one of the crowd members, in a ragged vest, trousers, and long wool shirt. His hair tumbled in loose strands to his shoulders.

"The king cannot arrest you all," he continued, gripping the onlookers with the strength of his voice. "And he cannot run his mines on his own. If you want to have a say in your government, you must speak together."

There was a rumbling among the crowd members.

"And who's to lead this group?" asked one man.

"We should have a meeting," said a woman.

"A meeting?" scoffed a man in a dark beard. "Lotta good that'll do! I'd say the time for talk is past."

Shouts erupted, and Aerin lost the thread of the discussion.

Then a sudden hush fell as a horse galloped into the square. A man in a plumed hat, ruffled shirt, and pair of silk trousers guided a tall black gelding up to the fringes of the crowd. There he paused, his elegant mount shifting his hooves in an uneasy manner. The man reached into a leather bag on the back of his saddle and lifted out a brown tube. "A correspondence for Mr. Antony Renning," he said.

Murmurs rippled in response, and rude comments sallied forth about the rider's fancy horse and clothing.

"And you are?" demanded the bearded man as he stepped forward from the crowd. He blocked the horse's path and crossed large arms over his muscular chest.

"Theodore Lorry, royal courier," said the man with the plumed hat.

Aerin felt a shudder run through her body. Even though she knew all this had happened long ago, she could not help but worry. Why would a royal courier have a message for her father unless the government was aware of his efforts to overthrow it?

A narrow gap opened between the rider and the podium. "I'm Antony Renning," said her father, without taking a step forward. "What do you want from me?"

The courier did not dismount, a move for which Aerin could not blame him. Instead, he steered his horse around the bearded man and urged the gelding to pick its way forward through the crowd. The horse did as it was told, snorting at anyone who came too close. At the front of the podium, the rider pulled on the reins, reached down to deposit the brown tube into Tony's hand, and stated calmly, "You've a summons from the princess."

Then the images began to dissipate. *No, no!* Panic rose in Aerin's throat. She had yet to learn the answer to her question. But the simulation had not come to an end, only that scene, and a new one was taking its place.

An elaborate room lit by a golden chandelier emerged before her. Carved oak chairs swept in a crescent around the room's edges. A polished desk served as the room's centerpiece, and sheets of paper with neat, curled calligraphy scattered the desk's surface. Two paintings hung on the walls, one of a beautiful pastoral setting and the other of an elderly man with a scepter in his hand. *The king,* Aerin supposed.

The lone window, set in a wall five feet thick, looked out over a courtyard. Her father stood gazing out, silent, his fingers clenching stone. His clothes were the same as he had worn in the last scene, though he had removed the ragged vest, tucked in his shirt, and bound his hair in a neat queue.

"So you are the one intent upon starting a war in my father's own city," a female voice came from the doorway. Tony whirled, and his jaw dropped at the sight of his accuser.

The young woman was unlike anyone Aerin had ever seen. Her chestnut hair coiled up around the edges of a silver circlet. Dark eyes glistened below a smooth forehead and arched eyebrows. A deep rose color spread over high cheekbones and pursed lips, and a dusky cinnamon gown clung to her curved shoulders before gliding to the floor.

Tony, having regained his composure, dropped his head in the slightest hint of a nod. "Your Highness," he said.

"Do take a seat, Mr. Renning." She gestured toward a chair. "I should not wish to have a lack of hospitality added to the list of faults you have leveled against my family."

He did not sit.

"Pray tell me, sir, how a young man from the Alliance came to care so much about disrupting the only planet in this region that cares to deal with the Council."

Tony gave a half smile. "I doubt Your Highness has any desire to hear the truth."

"On the contrary, I have been raised to listen to views beyond my own understanding." She crossed to the desk at the room's center, lifted an ink bottle, and placed it back down with a thud. "If I had not, you would be rotting away in a dungeon at this very moment. And the Alliance would have to manage without its most recent prodigy."

"I'm here on my own." Tony straightened his shoulders. "Not on behalf of the Alliance."

"So they would have us believe. According to the ambassador, if you return to Allied space, you will be sent to prison. Were you aware of this?"

His cheekbone twitched. "It is not unexpected."

"Tell me then." She turned the full power of those dark eyes upon him. "If you are not here to help the Alliance gain control of our supply of ironite, why are you trying to cause a rebellion on this planet?"

"Because the people of Mindowan deserve better."

The princess took a stutter step forward, then back, and her words when she spoke had lost their earlier tone of command. "Better than what, Mr. Renning?"

"Than years of hard labor in the mines so that others can enjoy the advantages of the metal they uncover."

Hard labor. A thousand memories from the fields of Vizhan scraped through Aerin's mind: the rips on her bare hands after weeding without gloves, the searing pain in her back and shoulders from working hunched over, the unrelenting heat bleeding her dry. Had her father been trying to save the people on this planet from the darkness of toil without hope? She had lived through that darkness. Its elimination she could defend.

The princess lifted a quill pen from the desk and ran her

fingers along the feathers. "We are in complete agreement on that. And what would you have my father do? Join the Trade Union?"

"The Trade Union is seeking power, not better lives for its people."

"Then I repeat, what would you have my father do? He has worked his entire life to keep Mindowan free from the Trade Union's control. I assure you, he did not go through all that effort only to have her swallowed up by the Alliance."

Tony's jaw tensed. "I'm not suggesting he give Mindowan to the Alliance."

Her eyes narrowed. "Then what are you suggesting?"

"That the people of this planet have the right to rule themselves."

The princess reacted to the statement, her quill pen falling to the floor. "And you believe that would work?" she asked softly.

"I believe the people must be given the chance."

"And you intend to help them achieve that chance?"

"Yes," he replied.

"Through violence?"

"Through words and conviction."

Slowly she retrieved the pen, her movement so smooth that not even her skirts rustled. For a moment Aerin could imagine the princess stretching out her finger in a gesture of command and ordering Tony's death upon the instant. But the forthcoming words surprised Aerin as they must have surprised her father. "Then I will arrange for you to speak with the king, Mr. Renning."

The simulation faded, the images disappearing without another word spoken. Aerin waited for a new picture to form, but none came. "It's done?" she murmured.

Dane stretched his arms behind his back. "It answered your question."

"No, it didn't. I asked—"

"Who your mother was. The computer answered."

Aerin's mind swirled. That beautiful woman with the royal bearing and aura of command? "She couldn't be my mother."

"She could," Dane said firmly. He stopped stretching and turned to face Aerin, his gaze intense. "You looked just like her at Christmas, in that red dress."

Aerin stared past the brown depths of his eyes. She had felt like royalty that night, like she belonged. And she could not have been more wrong. "Maybe the computer thinks I'm someone else. How can it know who I am?"

He broke the gaze. "It must have gleaned who you were when we were talking after the first scene. A simulator is designed to input data whenever it's running."

Could he not have mentioned that before? Now the machine would be able to trace her. But what did it matter in the face of all she had seen? Besides, she was already trapped here. She might as well take advantage of every moment.

"Simulator, my name is Aerin Renning. If that was my

mother, what happened to her?" It was such a vague question that as soon as Aerin had said it, she wanted to take it back; but the room was darkening, and there was nothing she could do but watch.

She felt Dane's arm slip around her waist.

They were in a small, simple room, dimly lit. Night had fallen. A woman in a homespun dress and a plain blue scarf crouched beside the fireplace. She rocked the sides of a cradle and hummed a soft melody. Her face glowed in the candle-light, the same face that had belonged to the princess.

It's true! Aerin realized. *This woman is my mother. And the baby in the cradle must be me.* Desperately, Aerin took in her mother's image, filling the void that had existed Aerin's entire life. While older than in the previous scene, the woman still looked young, no longer wealthy but in good health. Her dark eyes watched the door.

Then a fierce pounding vibrated its wooden boards. Aerin's mother leaped to her feet and flung up the latch. A man stood on the threshold, panting.

"Oh, it's you, Stephen." Disappointment rang heavy in her voice.

"Mrs. Renning," he said, struggling to catch his breath, "is your husband here?"

"No, Tony's out, waiting for the announcement."

"The announcement came, over an hour ago. I thought by now he'd be here to tell you."

"It's happened then? My father has signed over Mindowan

to its people? I knew he would. If anyone could win him over, Tony could."

"That's a lot of faith you have in your husband, Mrs. Renning, to give up everything to follow him."

"He's an easy man to follow, as I'm sure you know. Hasn't he led all the citizens of Mindowan to freedom this night?"

Pride burst through Aerin's chest. Her father had succeeded then!

Her mother gestured for the visitor to enter the room, but he shook his head.

"He has," Stephen replied, "but that's why I was searching for him. The crowds aren't out celebrating. They're storming the castle."

The swell of pride tumbled.

Fear threaded through her mother's voice. "What?"

"They're drunk, ma'am, and out to prove they've won. You know there were those who opposed your husband's negotiations with the king. They wanted action, not words. And after your marriage . . ."

"They broke away from Tony. But he was right. They must see that now. They have their freedom and without bloodshed."

"There's those who don't see it that way. They don't want a peaceful transfer of power. They want vengeance."

Aerin felt disappointment marred by fear. Was this what had happened to her father's dream? Her mother reached for a heavy wool shawl on a peg by the door. "Watch after Aerin, will you?"

"But I wanted to find your husband. He's the only one who can stop that mob."

She paused. "And they know that. They may have trapped him somewhere, or . . ." Her face drained of color, and she did not finish the statement. Instead, she brushed past the man in her doorway. "I have to go."

"No, ma'am, tell me where, and I'll look for him."

"I'm not going after Tony. I have to warn my father."

"But it's dangerous. I thought your father hadn't spoken to you since he disinherited you before your marriage. What if he doesn't listen?"

"He has to." She rushed off, disappearing into the night.

Aerin barely had time to assimilate the news that not only was she not royalty—a fact she had no trouble accepting— but that her mother had willingly forgone her own status in order to marry Tony. Why then—*why*—had he been so reluctant to mention her mother's name? Once again, the simulation shifted.

Pound. Pound. Pound. Almost a minute passed before Aerin could recognize her father in the darkness. He was hammering with a makeshift club against the inside of an old door, and she realized he must be trapped, as her mother had said. *Pound. Pound.* Then *crack!* The door split near the latch.

Tony attacked the weakness with ferocity, and the club did its job.

He shoved open the broken door and sprinted into the night without looking back. Shadows of wood buildings flashed past him on either side of the street. He took a corner, then another one, heading uphill. Twice he tripped over unseen obstacles, but he kept going, his breath now coming in heavy gasps. *He should be dead on his feet by now*, Aerin thought as he cut behind a merchant's shop and scrambled over a fence, then launched once again into a steady run.

The sky was beginning to lighten in the distance, and still he kept going. Now he was skirting the edge of a high stone wall, the silhouette of the castle in the background. The gate, torn from its hinges, lay on the ground.

Her father ran through the opening. No guards moved to block his path. Not a single person stood in the courtyard. Or at the castle entrance. Or the foyer.

Tony sped down a corridor littered with broken glass and skidded to a halt at the edge of a thick door. It was propped open. For a moment Aerin could see only him, not the room into which her father was staring. Then he sank to the ground.

And she saw what he did: the thick beams running across the ceiling, the ropes wrapped around the beams, and the figures dangling from the ropes—two bodies, their heads lolling against the knots that had severed their breath and ended their lives. That of an elderly man with white hair. And that of Aerin's mother.

Aerin's screams filled the Spindle's chamber. High-pitched panic slammed off the walls and echoed back at her, like a laser cutting into her skin and burning through her organs. She sank to the floor.

The simulation had long since come to an end, its final image searing her brain. What more was needed to make her father into the man she knew? A man, without passion or conviction, who lapsed into silence for hours at a time and had raised his daughter alone, outside the realm of any planet or political boundary.

Her lungs began to ache, but she could not stop the screaming. After years of horror, anguish had found a way out, and she could do nothing to curb its escape, would not have if she could.

Then warm arms circled her chest and rocked her back and forth. Dane was saying something. At first, the words failed to break through her emotion, but they continued, soft and steady, until she realized he was repeating the same line over and over. "You're all right. You're all right. You're all right."

She wanted to argue with him, to tell him she could not be all right, that she should *not* be. But the words tangled in her brain, and the screams drowned into tears. "I don't . . . I don't . . ." she choked.

"Don't what?" he whispered in her ear.

She was thinking of her mother. "I don't even know her name."

"Ilaina." It wasn't Dane who answered. "Or, more correctly, Her Royal Highness, Ilaina Seranee of Mindowan." And the rigid figure of Dr. Livinski stepped from the elevator.

Chapter Twenty-one
REPERCUSSIONS

DANE WAS LIVING ANOTHER NIGHTMARE. WITH THE echoes of Aerin's screams in the background and the images of last night drifting loosely through his vision; the penetrating stare of Dr. Livinski as she had stepped out of the elevator; the long, silent stretch of darkness on the ride down, down through the Spindle's stem, not to the hangar, but all the way down to the secret underground tunnel that led to the empty basement room of the Great Hall; the almost hollow shell that had been Aerin as she and he were escorted back to the dorm by the principal. And the love—yes, love—that had shown in his mother's eyes as she took his father's hand during the first simulation.

He tried to brush aside the visions. But the present experience of waiting for the beginning of the announcement ceremony was no more comforting. The hard bench dug repeatedly into his thigh as other first-years moved up and down restlessly. Voices swarmed over one another, and sweat was building up on the back of his neck, no doubt the result of the dense crowd packing the auditorium—fathers, mothers, grandmothers, grandfathers, brothers, sisters, aunts, uncles, and who knew who else—all eager to provide emotional support for their own Zack or Zelda. Dane's father had not come.

The principal moved to the front of the room with her thick stack of invitations for the lucky students who would be returning to Academy 7.

He would not be among them.

Don't care, he told himself. *Don't feel.*

He had known when he had agreed to take Aerin up to the Spindle that it would cost him. And it did not matter that he had yet to be punished. Because the woman standing at the podium with her head high, her neck stiff, was the same woman who had stared at him last night with that cold look of . . . disappointment. He didn't know how else to describe it. She controlled his fate, and he could do nothing to alter that imbalance of power.

Don't care, he reminded himself. Because if he didn't care, she couldn't hurt him.

But she could hurt Aerin. He could not shake the memory of Aerin's screams from his head. They had ripped through him, exploded out of her like the voice of insanity, and there had been nothing he could do. Nothing but hold her and lie to her by telling her she was all right.

He could not look at her now. Could not bear to see the blank gaze that had gone right past him when she had walked away from him last night.

"Ladies and gentlemen," Dr. Livinski's voice tore through the room, "welcome to the Academy 7 Announcement Ceremony."

The room sank into a brutal silence.

His heart spiked. Maybe this was why she had not punished him last night. Because she knew it would be more painful to live through the ceremony without hearing his name.

Don't. Care.

She began with the second-year students. The third-years would have their graduation ceremony later in the evening, a moment of pure celebration.

This. This was altogether different.

He had nearly forgotten that the second-years would be here, that they also had to be invited to return. There was no limit on the number of upcoming third-year students. They just had to satisfy Dr. Livinski.

A task, Dane knew, that was not worth taking for granted.

He listened with dull awareness as one by one the second-years rose to the sound of their names. The chosen students, smiles of relief spread across their faces, retrieved their envelopes and climbed the small staircase to the stage. A human line grew slowly until it covered the distance between the thick gathered curtains on either side.

The principal set down her remaining envelopes and clasped her palms together. "May I present next year's senior class."

Polite applause filled the room but faded rapidly beneath the rise in tension as the older students departed the stage. And the climax of the morning approached. Dane couldn't feel his hands. Or his feet. A strange, frayed breath filled his chest as the principal once again lifted an invitation.

And called a name. Not his. Or Aerin's. His soul emptied out, then refilled as she touched another envelope.

No, he ordered himself. *Don't hope.*

But again and again his chest rose and fell as the envelopes dwindled. Despite himself, he began counting the first-year students on the stage. "Twenty-one, twenty-two, twenty-three." *Only two spots left.*

But the names never came. Dr. Livinski was raising a hand, introducing the next year's class. Dane could not take in the words. Applause broke throughout the room. And the envelopes were gone.

Don't care. Don't feel. But it was much, much too late for that. Because he did care. It scared him how much he cared. And he did feel. He felt the muscle of his heart rip apart, and there was nothing he could do but watch it bleed all over the dreams he had never meant to have.

A piercing cry escaped from the end of the bench. Yvonne's.

It had not taken much thought to realize she had reported him last night to Dr. Livinski, but there was no satisfaction in knowing she also had failed to make the cut. Or that the final two spots, the ones the principal had chosen not to fill, had belonged to him and Aerin. Until last night.

The audience descended in a raucous swarm: rushing to comfort the rejected students and congratulate those on the stage. Swinging arms and shoving elbows jostled past. Legs scrambled over the bench, and voices clattered in his ears. He felt the approach of another person.

Aerin. He could not face her yet.

Then another shadow, this one he could not put off or avoid. Cold disapproval sliced the air as Dr. Livinski issued her stern directive. "Both of you. In my office. Now."

Chapter Twenty-two
COMMITTED

DANE FELT THE GLASS WALLS OF THE PRINCIPAL'S office close around him. He slumped down in a chair, letting the iron bars of its back dig into his spine and remind him where he was headed.

There was a prolonged silence.

Vaguely, Dane realized Aerin had yet to sit down. He reached for her hand, but she shook him off.

Dr. Livinski, also standing, began to reel off last night's crimes, counting deliberately with her fingers. "Trespassing, breaking and entering, illegal access to classified data—"

"It was my fault," Aerin blurted.

No! Dane tried to pull her down. *I'm the one with the record. Keep your mouth shut.*

But again Aerin rejected him. "It was my idea to break into the Spindle, not Dane's." She pulled free of his hand.

Chair legs scraped across the tiled floor as the principal slid into her seat, eyebrows arched. "Elaborate, Miss Renning."

Dane cringed. He could not expect Aerin to share the brutal account of her life. She had stripped herself emotionally bare last night, and he had seen the toll it had taken. But before he could open his mouth to argue, she began to talk. Her chin was up, her gaze level. The events were the same as those she had shared last night, but the words came faster, succinct, peeling from her lips with . . . confidence.

The principal interrupted only once, clearing her throat. "Indeed, I was made aware of your father's death just prior to Christmas. His ship was identified before it was crushed." She threaded her long fingers together. "Those of us on the Council held a meeting to listen to the *Fugitive*'s flight recorder."

Dane shuddered and closed his eyes. Then that explained the real reason why the General had returned and how he had known—known how and when Aerin's father had died. And known Aerin was lying. *He thought I was taunting him by bringing her home,* Dane realized, *that we both were.*

But Aerin did not allow the principal's revelation to interfere with her own. She tucked a strand of brown hair behind her ear, gave a brief nod, and began to talk about the tech lab break-in; then the flight through the spiral; and finally the simulations, ending with the stark description of her mother's death.

Dr. Livinski unthreaded her fingers and rubbed her forehead. "That entire rebellion." Anger grated through her voice. "Such a waste!"

Dane's eyes widened at the heartless comment. He had not considered the possibility that the principal might know more about the events surrounding the simulations. Her words from last night suddenly came back to him: *Ilaina Serranee*, Aerin's mother's name.

Of course Dr. Livinski knew more. She was on the Council. "Mindowan was swallowed up by the Trade Union," she said, then reached into her desk drawer and withdrew a thin black object. "The rebellion fell apart without Tony."

Tony? The informal name blared into the room.

And Aerin clutched the edge of the desk, then sank into the vacant chair. "You . . . you knew my father?" Her voice faltered for the first time throughout the confrontation.

There was a long pause as the principal ran a thumb across the edge of the rectangle in her hand, then flipped over the object.

To reveal a photograph.

Shock ripped through Dane's body. He had never seen the photo before, but he recognized every one of the four Academy 7 students in it: Aerin's father, wearing a wide, beaming grin; Dane's own father, less jovial, but still smiling; Dane's mother, so beautiful, so . . . happy; and the young woman from last night's simulation, the one who had remained on the couch throughout his father's argument with Tony. Dane raised his gaze slowly to the principal's face, then dropped it again to the young woman in the photo. The sharp features were the same.

"We were close," Dr. Livinski said, compassion exempt from her tone, "all of us." She paused. "At one time."

It had never occurred to him that she might have known his mother.

"You were there during the argument between my father and Dane's," Aerin whispered.

The principal tapped the edge of the picture, rocking it sharply. "And I would rather not have been. Gregory was furious." Her gray eyes flicked to Dane, then back to Aerin. "Of course, Tony might have broken the news more gently."

"Their friendship didn't survive?" Aerin asked.

"No," the principal said, "Gregory had just enlisted in the Allied Air Force, and he didn't do it lightly."

He never does anything lightly.

"When he enlisted, he committed his entire soul to the Alliance." Dr. Livinski swept the frame brusquely back into the drawer. "Tony never did that. To him, freedom was worth fighting for, but it was not inseparable from the Alliance. He believed the best place to make a difference was on a planet where the people couldn't obtain Allied support. Gregory never understood that"—she paused, then extended the thought—"though Emma did."

Something in Dane's chest tore at the sound of the name. Anger started to swell inside him. What gave this woman the right to have memories of his mother?

A brief shadow replaced the hard look in the principal's eyes. "I think Tony hoped she would change Gregory's mind. There was a lot more to Emma than her wealthy family. She was brilliant, you know."

The words burst from Dane before he could restrain them. "Then why did she marry my father?"

The principal blinked. "Your mother knew her own mind. She understood Gregory and smoothed over all his rough edges. Her parents didn't approve . . . so of course she married him, right out of school."

"I don't understand," Aerin broke in. "If she could have convinced him to forgive my father, why didn't she? What happened?"

A cold feeling developed in the pit of Dane's stomach.

The gray eyes flew to his face. He did not like those eyes. They saw too much.

"Emma died," the principal said. "She grew sick during her second pregnancy. The doctors treated her fever, but it left her very weak; and they suggested she abort the baby."

A shiver crept through Dane's skull. He had never heard the details.

"Gregory was away at the time," continued the principal. "He had been promoted only a few months before. When he learned she was sick, he tried to return home, but by then,

Emma was over the fever. She contacted him on board ship, told him not to worry, and let him think she had scheduled an abortion." *Let him think*: the phrase had a haunting ring.

"But she hadn't?" Aerin asked.

No.

Dr. Livinski answered her question but spoke directly to Dane. "Your mother never considered giving you up. She knew by the time your father returned to Chivalry, it would be too late to end the pregnancy, and she assumed she would have time to win him over to her way of thinking. But on his way home, your father's ship was detoured to Mindowan to remove Allied diplomats during the rebellion. When he arrived, Gregory tracked down Tony and tried to convince him to turn himself in. By that time, your parents and I had gained a certain amount of respect among the government. We would have testified on his behalf, but Tony refused."

"So it was my father's fault they never reconciled?" Aerin questioned.

The principal squared her shoulders. "Tony was a mess. He blamed himself for his wife's death, and Gregory knew that. He might have forgiven the argument. Except then Emma died."

"How?" Aerin whispered.

"I killed her." The words rushed from Dane's mouth before he could stop them. They slammed through the room, shattering like frozen fire.

The gray eyes were back on him as Dr. Livinski shook her head, something else joining the firm note in her voice. "She may have died giving birth to you, but it was her decision, her choice. The grief almost destroyed Gregory. He loved her so much he couldn't find it in himself to blame her, and he couldn't handle all the guilt himself so he spread it around. He blamed Tony and had him permanently exiled from the Alliance, charging him as a traitor and making him the scapegoat for the violence on Mindowan."

So Aerin's father also had been a victim of the General's anger.

"Why did we never learn this in school?" Aerin whispered. "Why is it classified?"

Dane knew the answer, but it was the principal who explained. She did not mince words. "Because the loss of Mindowan as a trade partner is the greatest setback the Alliance has faced in the past millennium. It empowered the Trade Union's sudden expansion, and at the time of the takeover, no one on the Council cared to publicly admit that the instigator behind the loss was a traitor."

"He wasn't a traitor!" Aerin's voice took on the fury it had held in her first debate.

"Perhaps not." Dr. Livinski buffeted the storm. "But he was an Allied citizen trained in our highest facility of learning. The Council had no desire to share that fact, and the current members, especially Gregory, have never been *compelled* to correct the story." The way she said the last sentence, leaning slightly forward, her gaze locked on Aerin's, made Dade shudder. It was a dare.

"My father did the right thing." Aerin stepped into the trap. "The citizens of the Alliance should know the truth."

She was correct, of course. Her father had not deserved to be targeted as the sole cause of the problems between the Alliance and the Trade Union. He had lived up to the ideals in the Manifest. And he could not have known his actions would end in disaster.

But neither should his daughter have to face the accusations that would come with the public release of what her father *had* done on Mindowan. "It's your secret, Aerin," Dane said. "You're the only one who needs to know."

"I'm not ashamed of my father." She met Dane's gaze. "Secrets have never done me"—*or you,* her eyes seemed to say—"any good."

Dr. Livinski leaned back, her hands resting on the stiff arms of her chair. "You insist on telling the public then."

Aerin straightened her spine. "I will if no one else will."

Thinly veiled satisfaction emanated through the principal's voice. "I will inform the rest of the Council of your decision, Miss Renning. I have no doubt the majority would prefer to release the classified files themselves, rather than wait to respond to a press conference. Gregory, of course, will be displeased."

Her attention turned to Dane. "Though your father was

not always so fond of secrets. Tony wasn't the only target of his anger after your mother's death. Gregory blamed me because I kept Emma's secret about choosing to have the baby." The gray eyes were direct. "And I'm afraid, Dane, that he blamed you."

She knew his father hated him. The knowledge made Dane almost physically ill.

"I should have realized there was something wrong when he tried to remove you from the school at the beginning of the year," the principal said, "but I just thought he was testing my authority. I turned him down"—she gave a wry smile—"and the next morning I woke up to a networking crisis." Her smile faded. "I assigned the two of you to work together, hoping you might form a connection and convince Gregory to finally forgive Tony. Of course, that was before I knew he was dead. I suppose I should have expelled you, but what would it have achieved except to unleash my most gifted students on an unsuspecting universe?"

Gifted? No one had ever called Dane that.

"Not every student has a plane in the hangar of the Spindle."

And there was the bitter crux of this conversation. In one brief comment, she had reminded him why he was here. He had broken the law, and she had the evidence she needed to convict him. Nothing else mattered.

"This school is the Alliance's future," Dr. Livinski continued, her hands curling tight. "It is about training leaders:

leaders who see past the problems and conflicts of today to find long-term solutions, leaders who take risks and set goals beyond current expectations, and leaders who defy what is safe or popular"—she eyed both Dane and Aerin—"to defend what is morally right."

The principal's next words demanded an answer. "Why did you come to this school, Dane?"

He struggled to speak, to say something, anything to defend himself, but the only words that came were the truth. "To get back at my father."

"And you, Aerin?" asked Dr. Livinski.

"I had nowhere else to go."

The principal paused.

Dane struggled against the silence. He tried to convince himself to form an argument before he ended up in prison, but all he could think was that he had already lost—his place here and, with it, his one shot at a future.

Dr. Livinski's next words confirmed his thoughts. "Neither of those reasons is good enough."

No, they were not. They were far from adequate. But he had been afraid to dream about staying. He had not known, when he came here, that she would stand between him and his father. Or that the teachers would encourage him to think for himself. Or that he would meet Aerin, whose problems were worse than his and whose will was stronger and who would make him wish he had a future in which he could get to know her better. Now it was too late.

"You have both done your best to throw away the opportunity of attending this school," the principal said. "And you
will not remain here as outsiders. This is not a place for hiding, or vengeance, or"—she wrinkled her nose—"snitches. If
you stay, you will do so as leaders."

Dane's head flew up.

"There *are* two remaining slots for students at Academy 7
next year." The principal held up a hand before either Dane or
Aerin could speak. "If you accept those places and fall short of
my expectations—which I assure you are astronomical—you
will be out of here at the speed of light. I want you both to
consider whether or not you really wish to return. This is a
choice. *You* must take on the responsibility for making it."

Reality whirled and collided within him. *His* choice. The
pulsing memories of the past year came to Dane all at once:
Pete's demand that the invitation was Dane's future and he'd
better pick it up; his father's accusation that Dane had cheated
and did not deserve to be here; and the principal's words from
only a few minutes ago—the words that had changed his life.
Your mother never considered giving you up.

That was something, wasn't it?

Aerin was watching him with riveted expectation.

"Are you staying?" he asked, not caring if she heard the fear
in his voice.

Her smile turned to a grin. There was a light in her face he
had never witnessed before. "Well, I can't very well leave the
future of the universe in your hands, now can I?" she teased.

Her eyes were glistening. *Joking.* Despite everything tragic she had learned about her parents, she had become more confident than he had ever known her.

"And you, Dane?" asked the principal. "Are you staying?"

"Yes," he said. And finally believed it.

Chapter Twenty-three
THE FOUNTAIN

AERIN SNUCK OUT THAT NIGHT. IT WAS SILLY, SHE supposed, as she slipped one leg over the windowsill and wrapped her hands around the solid branches of the maple tree. With the term officially over, there was no curfew. And no monitor on duty to keep her from simply walking down the stairs and out the main door.

But she had chosen to sneak out.

The graduation ceremony had run late into the evening, and while many of the students and their families had dispersed throughout the city, there were still too many in the dorm to ensure that her escape would go unnoticed. And she needed to complete this mission alone.

She eased her way down through the tangled branches, taking the time to enjoy their embrace and their strength.

By now each hand, each foothold was imprinted within her body so that she did not have to think about the mechanics of the climb. And while she took care not to evoke unnecessary sound, the threat of real danger had worn away. She was free to lose her thoughts in the night.

The crickets had tuned their calls, and the frog choir provided the melody. As she wove her way down, over one branch and under another, the song built to its vibrant climax, then timed its instant silence to match the final drop of her feet upon the ground. Aerin knew the choir would begin again within a moment; and sure enough, as she slipped into the garden's labyrinth, a single amphibian soloist reprised the opening notes of the song.

The trees welcomed her to their stillness. Heavy humidity had lurked over the day, and while the fall of the sun had eased the oppression, not even the tiniest wisp of a breeze rustled the leafy gowns of oak and cedar. Tonight the garden was at peace. Unlike last night.

Or perhaps the garden itself was not so different. Perhaps only her eyes and her heart had changed, in some ways and not in others. For hadn't the garden called her from the first day of her arrival? And hadn't the fountain, from the first time she had seen its sparkling shimmer?

She had answered dozens of times.

But this night she knew why.

The memory had come after the others, long after the first wave the night before in which she had opened the chest at the back of her mind, allowing herself to see all the moments with her father that had been pushing for attention these past seven years. The screams and tears that had blown through her at the sight of her mother's dead body had been shock, but they had also been a release. An unknown, unimaginable release.

It had been too hard, on Vizhan, to think about what she had lost. And after her escape, she had been afraid. But while the simulations had been filled with loss, anger, and death, they had also been filled with her father. And reminded her that he was none of those things. It had hurt, yes, to remember, but the pain had lessened with every memory. And by the dawn, Aerin had known she could survive.

The memory of the fountain had come later: this afternoon, once she was at peace. It had presented itself. Like a gift. She had seen her father, tall and firm, as he had looked to her when she was seven or eight. She had been angry with him because he had refused to answer her question about her mother.

He had taken her to a park on some planet whose name she could not remember and had led her up to the wide sunken basin of a fountain. Knowing he was trying to barter for her forgiveness, she had intended to sulk. But that fountain. It had felt huge, with its round rim and long sloping sides. There had been music. And color—bright green and pink and sharp blue that had danced in the streams of water.

But what she remembered most were the children: running

and shrieking and screaming as they dodged the rhythmic beams of spray in the inevitable hope of capture. Her father had motioned for her to join the boys and girls with their sopping clothes and wild movements. And she had wanted to. *Oh, she had wanted to!*

But she had been scared. The other children had brothers and sisters and friends, someone else with whom to play. Her father had offered to go down to the water with her, but none of the other children had fathers holding their hands.

And she had said no.

He had been hurt. The look in his eyes had shown that he believed she was rejecting him. She had not meant to, but she was too ashamed to admit her fear. Instead, she had sat with her father in silence for a long time at the top of the basin. And envied those children running and playing and laughing in the water.

He had never taken her back to that park.

And she had never asked about her mother again. But neither had Aerin ever explained to him about her fear at the fountain. Never apologized. And perhaps never forgiven him for not telling her the entire truth.

Maybe that was why she had not wanted to remember. Not only because she was afraid of feeling the raw agony of his loss, but because she was ashamed that, despite his death and all his love, she had failed to forgive him this one thing.

Until last night. When she had finally understood why he had not told her about her mother. Because he had loved her, loved her too much to talk about her, and loved Aerin too much to share with her the pain of his grief.

And now she could think of only one way to apologize.

I'll make you proud, she told her father in her thoughts. *I'll prove to them all that you taught me well, that you were loyal to the ideals of the Manifest, and that I belong here in the Alliance.*

She believed that now. Though it had not been the knowledge that she was a citizen that had changed her feelings. It had been her father's idealism and her mother's bravery. It was their legacy that had given Aerin the confidence to accept Dr. Livinski's offer to return. And it was that legacy she must embrace.

The fountain was waiting for her. It had no fluorescent lights or hidden speakers, but it had color, the deep misty green of Academia's night and the glittery sparkle of reflected moonlight. The frogs and crickets still sang, their music joined by the ever present *shhh* of the water's spray.

She stretched out her hands, fingers first, letting them disrupt the perfect flow. Her palms opened and closed, striving to capture the streaming essence, but the cool liquid spilled down her wrists and arms instead, dripping into pools beneath her elbows.

And then she stepped into the downpour, closed her eyes, tilted up her face, and thought with reckless abandon, *I am not afraid.*

$\mathcal{E}$pilogue: PUNISHMENT (REPRISED)

"Dane," Aerin said as she balanced on the scaffolding. The boards felt warm under her bare feet, and the high sun beat down on her forehead. Her hands tapped the rails running the length of the black tube in front of her. The spiral of the Spindle. Unmoving. "I think we may have underestimated Dr. Livinski."

"What gives you that idea?" he said over the whirr of the handheld slicer as he guided it through the ironite surface. "That she caught us every time we broke the rules, or that she has us providing her with free labor thousands of feet above the ground." He curved the Ephesian slicer to the edge and watched the chunk of solid black material fall into the catch basket.

Aerin pulled in the basket, checked the hooks on the pulley system, and let the container sail down toward the ground. She ignored his lame complaint. "The fact that she created a punishment that helps us all."

"Oh really?" Dane flipped off the switch. The *whirr* subsided as he hung the lightweight tool on a nearby pole. "And what," he said, hefting their lunch box onto his shoulder, "is so great about spending our summer deconstructing this spinning death threat?" He grasped the rails of the scaffolding and ascended the side of the spiral, failing to wait for an answer.

Aerin climbed up beside him, securing a perch on the sloping ironite.

He settled the lunch box by the railing and handed her a water bottle. She grappled with him over an apple, lost the fight, and snagged a nectarine instead, then returned to the earlier thread of the conversation. "Well, from Dr. Livinski's perspective, she gets to have us clean up our fathers' mess."

Dane groaned. "I should have known this tube was the brainchild of my father's insanity." He took a bite of the prized apple and frowned at it.

Aerin grinned, glad that he could now talk about his father. According to the principal's grudging admission, the Spindle's blueprint had been the senior project for her and her once close-knit friends. The simulator had been Emma's invention; the elevator, Dr. Livinski's, and Dane's and Aerin's fathers were to blame for the moving spiral.

"You know none of them ever meant to place anyone in danger," Aerin reminded him. "They thought the tube would deter people from trying to enter the Spindle. After all, who would be reckless enough to fly into such a thing?" She ducked as Dane hurled the apple at her.

"As I was saying," he said, "how does Dr. Livinski's order to dismantle this deathtrap help *us*?

"We get to stay here all summer," Aerin replied. "Neither of us has to find a place to live or a short-term job."

"Right, because working thousands of feet above the planet's surface is such a cushy position, we wouldn't want to give that up."

Aerin leaned back on one hand and took a bite of the soft nectarine. Its rich juice drizzled over her tongue. She stretched out her bare feet in the sun and let them enjoy its healing warmth for several minutes as she dropped her gaze to the scene below, not the Great Hall or its surrounding lawn, but beyond the outer wall to the mile upon mile of city buildings, parks, libraries, and bookstores—just waiting to be explored. "At least we're free to travel beyond the Wall," she said, "all summer long. And we don't have anyone to supervise our work."

"You're right." Dane drew closer, the shade of his brown eyes changing. "That is a plus." He leaned forward, hair falling in front of his eyes, and lowered his mouth as though to kiss her.

Then stopped, his eyes asking permission.

The sun's rays radiated up from her feet, through her legs, her arms, her face. There was no shudder, no chill, no irrepressible desire to flee. She linked her hands behind his neck, pulling his mouth close. And felt the warm taste of certainty as her toes curled beneath her.